Time in a Little Blue Bottle

Her fantasies fulfilled

Dani Haviland

USA Today Bestselling Author

Time in a Little Blue Bottle is a work of fiction. Names, place, characters, and incidents are the product of the author's imagination and are used for the readers' enjoyment. Any resemblance to persons living, dead, or fictional, events or business establishments is entirely coincidental.

Book Description

Isabella would do anything to rescue her sister from the den of Lionel the Loanshark but didn't realize she would have to deal with Mark Twain, Elvis, a vampire, a teenage boy who had a crush on her, and a trip to Australia. Would she be able to retrieve the precious bottle of Fountain of Youth water there? And did her sister really want to be rescued?

Reconnect with a few of your favorite time travelers from The Fairies Saga and meet new heroes and hiss at new villains in this bright and unusual Happy Ever After tale.

Dedicated

This story is dedicated to Marsha Renfro, a wonderful woman and mother who suggested the name Bella for the beautiful girl on the cover. She lost her own Bella much too early. I can never replace your daughter, Marsha, but know her name is being honored in this story.

Chapter One
In London
With Elvis and Company

Rare Arts and Antiquities Emporium
January 31, 2015

The academic investigators who practically lived in the Emporium's windowless low-ceilinged room paid no attention to the odd lot of men gathered in the corner. They were passionate about their own studies and didn't have any interest in the long-haired old men in period costumes or the celebrity impersonators who hovered near them.

Suddenly, as if led by an orchestra conductor, everyone in the room looked up—not a mumble or whisper was uttered—then they returned to their hunched-over postures and resumed their research, not knowing or caring what had happened.

But some realized the air was different now, enlivened. The atmosphere of the sub-basement area was now brisk, no longer musty or devoid of energy, but alive, almost electrically charged. A few of the scholars looked around to see what had happened. The others—more intent on their studies—simply sniffed the air for smoke or a gas leak, then returned to their yellowed tomes.

A new patron stood just beyond the old men in the archives section. His tall broad-shouldered stance looked out of place among the others. His arrival down the rickety, threadbare carpeted stairs had not been heard nor seen, but he was certainly the center of attention now for all but the most grizzled academics.

"Wh...why are you here, Cleveland?" Leonardo da Vinci the elder asked, subconsciously pulling his loosely knotted cravat up over his billowy ivory shirt. *Why would the Prime Vampire be here today? Or ever?*

Cleveland smiled at his former protégé. "Do I need a reason?"

The fixation on the tall newcomer wasn't just the result of his sly grin or Olympic swimmer body build. When he spoke, everyone in the musty alcove gazed at him in fascination, as if he was about to share the secret of how to make a million euros without breaking a sweat or a law.

Leonardo cleared his throat and blinked erratically as he

tried to erase his nervous smile. "No, no. You're just as welcome here as anyone else. I was just wondering if you needed some help with research. As you know, my associates and I have a lot of experience..."

Cleveland laughed without constraint, causing the young blonde librarian who had been watching the dark-skinned demi-god to drop her armload of papers. She quickly gathered them together, then hid under the work center table to listen in on their conversation.

"No offense, Leo, but I think I have more 'experience' than five of you put together."

"At least," Leonard the elder agreed. "Sorry. I meant no disrespect, sir. That being agreed upon, if there is anything you require, please, do not hesitate to ask."

The full-lipped man with the black pompadour nudged the sixty-ish Southern gentleman next to him. "Who's he, Twain?" he drawled.

"Sakes alive, Elvis, didn't you pay attention? They gave us a whole week of training about Cleveland before we could move up to the next level."

"Um, I must have overslept that week. Or maybe that was just for you folks from the 1800s. We only learned about current, important stuff," Presley said, then ran his fingers behind his ear, making sure he still didn't have a hair out of place.

"Horse feathers! I know they still teach about the vampire who saved—or changed, depending on your point of view—Alexander the Great." The white-haired, but still robust author twisted up the ends of his mustache. "Kids! You buy them books, teach them to read, learn them a job, and still they just lollygag around, dandying themselves up for the ladies."

"Hmph. I'll bet there's nothing he can do that I can't do better," Elvis said, then punctuated his remark with another snort of disgust.

All the other time travelers hurried to 'shush' the impetuous newcomer, but it was too late. Cleveland had heard Elvis.

"Since your education was neglected—and I don't see how they let you out of the primary classes with that attitude—I'll give you a short lesson. I can hear better than any animal around, so be careful what you say, even if you're in the next room; I can see further than any of Galileo's telescopes," he nodded to the 15th century sage at the far side of the round table, "and I can jump higher than any frog

4

in Calaveras County…or any other animal that has ever existed."

Elvis gulped hard but didn't even try to speak.

"But you're right. There's one thing you can do that I can't…" Cleveland paused for effect, then said, "I can't put on mascara."

Elvis pulled his chin in, embarrassed that the secret to his beautiful blue eyes was being so blatantly dismissed.

"You see, I can out-perform any man, past or present; am stronger than any vampire who ever existed; I can even walk in the noonday sun, but I'll be damned if I can see my reflection in a mirror!"

All the men in the area laughed along with Cleveland. The Prime Vampire knew they all feared him, but he'd like to think that he could still make a joke out of his one limitation.

Cleveland turned away to look at the two men across the room, and the nervous laughs stopped abruptly.

"Actually, I'm here for a reason. I need to make sure your short-statured associate doesn't make a mistake with that man," and nodded to the two men seated at a corner table, intent on the contents of a small tin.

"Simon?" asked Michelangelo. "He's harmless. He gets a

bit overwhelmed at times, but he means no ill will. He should learn how to defend himself better, though. Just recently—a year or two ago—he was beat up and robbed of his map. He managed to sort it out without any permanent harm done, but he's been a bit skittish ever since."

Cleveland turned his gaze back to the balding genius. "Any permanent harm…yet."

"Oh, no, sir. I promise you. Simon is a crusty sort, but he's just a traveler, and only an observer at that. Oh, and I have no idea who that…that day walker is."

"That, dear Michel, is no day walker. That is Marty Melbourne. He may look inauspicious, but I guarantee you, what transpires between those two will make or break a country. A large country. A water-locked country…"

"You're talking about Australia, aren't you?" Mark Twain asked. "I've been there. It's in no danger. Those folks are a tough bunch."

Cleveland shook his head. "Now *you're* the one talking like a day walker. You were there when? Late 19th century?"

Mark Twain nodded, too angry and embarrassed at Cleveland's righteous admonishment to speak. Australia was a new colony—relatively speaking—when he had first visited it in 1895. He had returned as a time traveler only a few years ago. He still found it hard to believe so much could change in a century. It rarely happened that he thought of time in a linear fashion. He'd been a time traveler for over a hundred years, but occasionally forgot how time—easily bent or pulled aside for travelers like those in his elite group—could be permanently creased or torn, thus causing a rift in the time space continuum and creating an alternate 'now.'

Cleveland returned his attention to Michelangelo. As if he could read his mind—and he could—the tall, dark potential menace answered the scientist/artist's unspoken question. "This man's legacy—the Melbourne Legacy—needs to be protected. You do know what a Möbius strip is, don't you?"

Michelangelo shook his head in frustration, then looked to the most affable in the group for help.

Twain sighed, then rolled his eyes. Time to teach the teacher. Again. He grabbed a strip of paper from the trash next to the copier, gave it a half twist, then taped the joined edges together. "Look, Mike, I'm sure you've seen this before, but it was only recently—relatively so—that it was named." Twain pulled a pen from the cup on top of the printer. He put pen to paper and drew a continuous line.

"See? I didn't lift the pen, essentially marking on only one side, but still, I've drawn on both—two—sides."

"And that is the Melbourne legacy. In this timeline—which we must maintain—James Melbourne is born in the 20th century. However, he lives out his life, and makes grand contributions and changes in the 18th century, and eventually dies, in the 19th century. The son of that man—that pushy, busybody Marty Melbourne—*has* to be found and protected by a friendly local, so to speak, after he arrives in Australia with The First Fleet in 1788. We can't let his father find him and bring him back to this time, the 21st century. James Melbourne may have been born to live out his life in this era, but that is not his destiny. Too many lives in Australia—then and now—depend on him *not* returning."

Michelangelo shook his head. *He didn't care what happened to anyone named Melbourne, or to Terra Incognita—or Australia or whatever they called that oversized island now.*

He also didn't care if he was upsetting Cleveland, this statuesque male with the most perfect body he'd ever seen. He was tired of staying alive. Death was part of living, and he had been ready to check out for decades, maybe even centuries: he'd lost track. He'd have gladly succumbed to the peace of death long ago, but Leonardo, Senior kept pushing the Fountain of Youth tonic on him, either blatantly in a toast, or slyly, in his cup of evening wine.

However, if he could get this tribute to the male form to pose for a painting—or maybe indulge him even more on a personal level—he'd be willing to hang around for a few more centuries. It didn't matter to him whether Cleveland was human or vampire. Either way, he was indeed 'prime.'

Chapter 2
In Liverpool
With the Spy Kid

Same date, place, and time

The curly-haired blonde chewed on her thumb knuckle as she studied the gathering of oddly dressed men. *What did they say? Could it really be? Could that black Adonis be a vampire? He was too dark to be a real one. Weren't they all supposed to be pasty white with coal black hair? This one was cappuccino brown with golden dreadlocks. He looked like a Reggae artist, not a blood sucker.*

And that man with the outrageous sideburns said he's the real Elvis, the King of Rock and Roll. I thought Elvis got fat and died. No way! And that other guy who looks like he should be on TV—selling fried chicken or used cars—can't really be Mark Twain. If he was, he'd have to be two hundred years old, at least.

Cleveland turned and smiled in the direction of the nervous young woman studying him and his protégés. He closed his eyes and inhaled her aroma. She was barely out of her teens and still a virgin. A man would be lucky to have a young woman so pure and healthy as his wife, but he'd need to keep her close. This one was high spirited and impetuous—and was on the prowl for either goods or information. She was either a thief or a spy. Or both!

The waif with wheat-chaff blonde hair groaned softly in embarrassment and returned a weak smile to the supposed vampire. She remained huddled under the table, doing her best to be invisible, shuffling the papers she had just picked up, piling them on top of her ancient text. She'd pretend to put away books later. Right now, she wanted to hear more of their conversation. These just might be the men Lionel was referring to.

Cleveland forced down the hint of a smile that arose as he recalled his first crush, a fair-haired peasant girl who carried sacks of fresh goat cheese for sale. This girl didn't look quite like Katrina, but she did have that same aura of innocence mixed with a determination to succeed, not for her own personal gain but to help others. He scowled as he recalled how getting involved with Kat had soured. She had betrayed his trust and as a result, he had lost his human, warm-blooded life. His feet tingled in recall of being burned at the stake as a heretic, her father standing in the crowd, laughing at him, showing off the purse of coins he had received as bounty for turning him in. And Katrina, cowering at her father's side, her swollen and battered face devoid of emotion, glassy-eyed in shock at what she had done. Those with family in need were the most dangerous sorts. Katrina had betrayed him to help her father, although by the looks of her bruised countenance, she hadn't offered up the information willingly.

Cleveland sensed that this twenty-first century look-alike to his first love, this *bella regaza innocente,* no longer had parents but did have family in peril. He would gladly watch out for her, but from afar. He wouldn't put himself in the position to get burned again—his skin with holy water or his icy heart with the warmth of love.

Then there he was, standing in front of the table she had hidden beneath, his decision to watch her from afar overridden by his desire to help a damsel in distress. "Come out, young one," he said, and stepped back, allowing her plenty of room to crawl out from underneath.

"You're not going to hurt me, are you?" she asked.

He shook his head, his amber dreadlocks glistening gold

in the dim incandescent light from the sconce on the wall. Then he offered his hand.

Don't fall for that! He's a vampire! Don't touch him or you could be turned into one, too! "Um, I can manage," she said, then clutched the book on medieval science to her chest and crawled on two knees and one hand to make her way out.

"What is your name, mistress?" Cleveland asked, bringing both hands behind his back. *She must have heard our conversation. She knows what I am and is afraid of me, even my touch.*

"My name is Izzy," she said, and wrapped her other arm around the tome, protecting her heart and other soft parts from the mead-colored vampire with the thick book. "I mean, it's really Isabella, but my sister and classmates call me Izzy."

"Ah, Bella. The name means beautiful, as indeed you are. Your parents chose your name well; your sister and classmates…" He shrugged one shoulder and wrinkled his nose in mild disgust, "Not so much. Now, what can I do for you today, Bella?"

"Uh, I don't need anything. I was just making some copies of this book when I dropped some of the papers. I was just picking them up when…"

"I'm sorry we frightened you. My friends and I are members of a traveling theater ensemble. They do look rather spectacular, don't you think?" Cleveland turned to the other members of his troupe and stifled a chuckle. They were still arguing about whether the women in Paris or Venice were more appealing and of which era. Michelangelo, however, was turned away from the conversation, still staring at him. *Still infatuated with me after all these years...*

"You didn't scare me," she lied, standing up straighter so she didn't look so timid. "I'm just clumsy. All the time clumsy... I'd better get back to work. These books won't shelve themselves," she said, adding a nervous chuckle.

"The name is Cleveland. If you need assistance, in anything at all," he said, his eyes fixed on hers, "Just call my name. I have *extremely* sensitive hearing."

"Yes, sir, I mean, yes, Cleveland." She turned to leave, then couldn't help but turn back to him, her timidity suddenly replaced by boldness. "And thank you for the new name. I like Bella. It makes me feel—I don't know exactly the right words—but stronger, more capable."

"You're welcome, sweet Bella. Farewell." He nodded to her to her, then added softly, "For now."

Bella walked away from the gathering of odd men. Whether they were impersonators, actors, nuts, or famous people out of time she'd probably never know. Whoever they really were, one thing was certain: they were intense. Their personalities were so dynamic, this section of the library was positively heady with emotional perfume.

And Cleveland—he was at least three levels above intense. How could someone pull off being sexy and frightening at the same time, but also feel like he was now her protector? Call him if she needed help? Lord help whoever had to face that big man. Or vampire or whatever he was. Just the sight of him enraged would probably scare off the most malicious foe. And Lord help *me* if I'm ever in a situation where I have to call a vampire for help!

Eager to leave the carnival of characters and get fresh air and a coffee, Bella knew that if she didn't get something of value, either tangible goods or information, that slug of a pimp Lionel would kill Phoebe. It would have to be information, though, because these books were too big to spirit out in a backpack, even if she knew which ones were the most valuable.

"Lots of interesting sorts spend time in those fancy bookstores and libraries you're so fond of," Lionel had told her. "No one knows or cares if you actually work there. One of these days, you'll hear information valuable enough to me that I'll let your sister go. In the meantime, Phoebe's mine to use as I wish. She's going to work off her debt to me one way or the other. And as long as her looks stay decent and she doesn't protest too much, she'll keep breathing."

Then the once popular heavyweight boxer leaned into her face, his greasy dark locks falling forward, his bloodshot eyes glistening with anger, ready to dish out another portion of intimidation. "But know this, runt: my tastes shift quickly. Just because your sister satisfies my appetite today doesn't mean I'll tire of her by morn. You're plain enough that no one will remember your face. You'll blend right into those dusty bookshelves. You'll know who to hover near when you see him. Or them. They rarely travel alone."

"Looks like I found the motherlode," Isabella whispered to the ancient book of alchemy she held as a prop. "Now let's see if I can fly away from my iron-shackled life with gold-dusted wings and set Phoebe free."

As she wove her way through the massive bookshelves

toward the stairs, Isabella heard the two men at the corner table, the name Melbourne rising like a whiff of cinnamon, calling her to them. *Shoot! Cleveland was telling the old coots about the Melbourne Legacy. These must be the two men he was referring to. I'd better find out more.*

As casually as she could, a cold sweat rising on the back of her neck, Isabella set her book on the shelf of the bookcase closest to the pair. She pulled out a couple of books at eye level and peered through the opening at the short bald man in a black frock coat and the tall silver-haired gentleman pushing a small tin toward him. Front row seat. She couldn't have paid for a better view.

***

Isabella knocked lightly on the frame of the doorway, then gingerly pulled back the beaded curtains. She knew Lionel was aware of her presence. He had security cameras everywhere and monitors plastered all over the walls in his 'Den of Pleasure,' as he called it. It had to be more like a 'Chamber of Horrors' for poor Phoebe.

She took two steps inside the room, then froze. Her eyes shifted away from her scantily-clad sister, not wanting to see the sinful and despicable nature of her existence. If this information was valuable enough, she could buy Phoebe's release from the clutches of this middle-aged pot-bellied curmudgeon.

Isabella cleared her throat and clenched her fists, willing herself to speak without faltering. "I believe I have information that will be of interest to you, valuable enough that you'll let my sister go."

Lionel looked up from his reclined position on the pile of oversized pillows, his hand resting on Phoebe's lingerie-covered breast. He gave his favorite consort's nipple a pinch, causing her to squeak, then stifle a giggle. She wasn't supposed to let Izzy know that she enjoyed her captor's attention. As long as little sister thought she was a sex slave and not a willing partner, the gullible girl would spend hours at the library and other stuffy dens of learning, looking for the rarities that afforded her insatiable and very capable lover his lavish lifestyle. Hopefully Izzy really had found something today. Lately, the information coming through to Lionel from his multiple sources had been old or of little use, and he was getting cranky. If he lapsed into a down and out foul temper, he was likely to take it out on her with his fists. He always apologized and lavished gifts and attention on her afterwards, but she'd have to endure being his punching bag first. Then again, a new bracelet would be nice.

"Spit it out, runt!" Lionel bellowed. "I don't have all day!" He reached down and cupped Phoebe's fanny and began massaging it, working her flesh back and forth with his big chunky fingers and thumb. "I have *big* plans for your sister here, and they don't involve an audience. This time."

Isabella swallowed the groan that always came unbidden when Lionel referenced having sex with her sister. She wanted to believe that Phoebe was being strong—tough for her, bearing her burden bravely so she wouldn't feel guilty that she had screwed up and made her a prisoner when she couldn't repay Lionel the Loanshark. Other times, it looked as if her sister actually enjoyed that moldy old fart's grabs and pinches.

"Just a few minutes ago, in the basement of the Rare Arts and Antiquities Emporium, there was a gathering of old men in long robes—they looked like they were on break from a Passion Play or something. A couple of celebrity impersonators were with them also. They were talking about two old men going to Australia to make sure that some Melbourne Legacy didn't get corrupted."

She closed her eyes, realized that what she had just said sounded lame, even to herself. It had sounded so much better when she heard it in person.

"And…" Lionel boomed, holding back his elation. This is exactly what he'd been waiting for, but he couldn't let her know that.

"And something about two timelines and the space time continuum. There was also some other Star Trekkie-type name—monotonous or something like that."

"Could it have been Möbius?" Lionel asked, then held his breath. *This was too good to be true!*

"Yes, I'm sure that's what it was," she answered, then bit her bottom lip nervously and looked toward the doorway, eager to get the transaction concluded. *He doesn't need to know about the vampire! He's already excited about whatever that Möbius deal was. I need to keep the information on the vampire as an ace up my sleeve in this poker game he's playing with my sister as the pot.*

Lionel couldn't contain his excitement and elbowed up into a sitting position, Phoebe falling to the side with her loss of physical support.

"I'll tell you what. What you've brought me today has

potential, but it's not the whole story. I need to have everything—not just a tidbit—before I'll free your sister." He shifted his silky loungewear and leaned forward, his elbows on his knees, posturing himself to make intimidating eye contact with the headstrong young woman. When she wouldn't return his gaze, he resorted to calling her out.

"Look at me when I'm talking to you, girl!"

Bella turned her shoulders toward him but kept her eyes low. *Ugh! How can I un-see that!* Her neck snapped up and she looked him in the eyes. Anything was better than seeing his exposed lumpy and wrinkly man parts.

Lionel looked down and saw that his excitement had poked through his sarong. "You like that, do you? Well, if you bring me what I want, I'll give you a taste of *el serpiente,*"

Without thinking, big sister Phoebe reached up and smacked Lionel on the shoulder with a jealous punch. "That's not what she wants," she said, biting off the words, 'she's still a virgin.' That surely would have excited him and been a certain way for him to bring her to his bed. It's not that she still cared to protect her little sister—it's just she didn't want to share Lionel's affections with anyone else.

"Worthless, get in here," Lionel shouted toward the

hallway.

Bella glanced sideways as a slight young man—just a few inches taller than she was but lithe and reedy—approached. She'd never seen him around. All the men Lionel surrounded himself with were oversized in body bulk and under-equipped in brain power. This one looked like a chimney sweep who had never aged, small in stature but with a twinkle of street savvy in his eye.

"Yes, sir," the youth said, his hands lax at his side, his head bowed in submission, hiding his glint of rebelliousness.

Worthless? What a horrible name! Bella stepped aside so the young man could be the center of Lionel's attention.

"You have a new job. I want you to be Izzy's escort. It's not that I don't trust her, but I don't trust her. Plus, she's going to need a few items, and you're the one who's going to procure them for her."

"Why me? You know I have finals…"

"You don't need to go to those ridiculous classes. I can set you up with whatever degree you want. But what I need is more of this." Lionel pulled a small blue bottle out from under one of his pillows, a travel-sized container of bellyache medicine. "And I want it filled to the top with the elixir of life."

"You want milk of magnesia? I can get a bottle of that from any chemist in town."

"I don't want this stuff," Lionel shook the vial in the air, "or the vial it's in."

"All right. I'm confused," the young man said. "If it's the wrong one, why do you keep that old bottle of antacid so close?"

"Because I figure if I hold onto it and visualize the right one, I'll get it. Now, stop being so nosy, Worthless!"

Bella visibly cringed at Lionel's rant and saw it had the same effect on the man it was directed at.

"Sorry. What does she need?" he asked, still not acknowledging she was in the same room.

"I don't know yet. She said there were some eccentrics talking about two old men going to Australia. She'll need tickets for the same flight as the old coots. Plus, you'll have to go with her. No telling what she'll need when she gets there."

"Does she have a passport?"

"Hell, how would I know? You're the facilitator. Either search her backpack or ask her—your choice. She's standing right next to you."

"Anything she needs?" he asked, stifling his excitement of getting *carte blanche* for this mission.

"Anything," Lionel said, then shifted back into his reclined position. He put his hand back on Phoebe's breast. "We'll stay busy while you two find the real little blue bottle. And make sure it's at least half full. You know what I'm talking about, Worthless. I'll kill you this time if you steal it from me again."

"Yes, sir," he said, then turned to his new charge. "Come on. We have lots to do."

Bella realized she had been biting on her thumb knuckle—again—and pulled it out of her mouth and followed. She'd play the meek and mild *femme* for a while. Shoot, who was she trying to fool? She *was* the meek and mild young woman, ignorant of life on the street. She'd learned a few survival skills since her sister had disappeared out of her life, but they were just that: for survival. Don't look anyone in the eye, never speak up, walk with a beaten down posture, blend into the surroundings. Petty theft was necessary, but she only stole enough to feed herself and keep herself warm. Shelters didn't care if you gave a real name or not, and because she kept her own blanket in her backpack, she didn't have to worry—much—about lice or bed bugs.

She brought her head up when she realized she missed something. "I'm sorry. Were you speaking to me?"

"Nope," he said, "but now that you're aware and not lost in your own little world, do you care to tell me what's going on?"

"Can I know your name first? I'm sure it's not Worthless."

He chuckled and shook his head. "Lionel expanded my childhood nickname of Wort into Worthless. Wort is short for Arthur, but I prefer Artie."

"Oh, yeah. I remember Wort from that King Arthur movie when I was a kid." Isabella smiled as she recalled watching movies on video tape while her older sister babysat her. The chilly basement they shared with their single mother wasn't much of a home, but at least they had electricity, a vintage TV-VCR player, and a collection of videos to keep them distracted.

"There you go again," Artie said, "off in your own little world. If I'm going to help you, I need to know a few things first. Do you have a passport?"

"Nope. I'll save you some time. All I have are the clothes I'm wearing and a backpack with a few snack bars, a water bottle, and a blanket in it. I travel light," she said, trying to turn her grimace of poverty into a chic smile of being cool and continental.

"Or you're a lousy thief."

"More like someone who doesn't care to steal more than she needs to survive. Now, are we going to discuss my personal ethics or figure out what we need to do so I can get my sister away from that creep?"

Artie swallowed his shock. Evidently she didn't know that Phoebe wasn't a captive, but was head over heels in lust with his gross older brother. "So, Phoebe's your sister?" he asked.

"Yes, she is. She practically raised me. I was only twelve when our mother died. Even before that, she was the one who raised me 'cause Mom worked all the time."

"You mean she reared you. People raise corn and puppies; they rear children."

"I heard you and Lionel talking about school. So, does this mean you're one of those insufferable college kids?" she asked with a barely contained sneer.

Kid! I'm thirty years old! "No, I'm not. Sorry if I came off as rude. If we're going to be working together to gain your sister's freedom, we need to at least be civil. Can we start all over again?"

"All right. I'm Isabella, but my sister always calls me Izzy. I don't really care for it, though." She stood up straighter as she remembered the 'power' name Cleveland had given her. "I prefer the name Bella. As far as what Lionel is so excited about, earlier today, I overheard several old guys plus Elvis and Mark Twain talking about Möbius and time space continuum stuff. If I get more information about whatever that is, that fat hairy pig will let my sister go."

"First off, Elvis and Mark Twain are dead."

"Yeah, that's what I thought, too." Bella hefted her backpack over her shoulder. "But if they are, they're bathing in some mighty potent pickle juice. They'd earn top money as celebrity impersonators with the way they look and talk. I didn't hear him sing, but that guy had the same satiny smooth voice as Chad Gates in Blue Hawaii, my favorite musical of all time."

"Great, just what I needed," Artie mumbled under his breath. "To get hooked up with an Elvis fan." He sighed loudly and spoke up. "Come on. We need to pick up the trail of the two men you said were going to Australia. I need to find out which city they're flying into so I can tap into the airline's reservation system, then book tickets for us on the same flight and in nearby rows. I hope they're going first class. That's a long flight."

"Um, I have a confession to make…" Isabella said. "I didn't tell Lionel everything."

"Yeah, so? That makes you smarter in my book," Artie said, a smile arising on his whiskerless face. "You have to hold back from him, so you always have just a little bit more valuable, or even trivial, information. I'd prefer you didn't hold back from me, though. I'm not the one holding your sister hostage. I'm the one helping you get her back. What might seem insignificant to you might mean something to me. So, spill."

"The men are called Master Simon and Lord Martin Melbourne. They want to leave in two days and this Simon guy wants to travel first class. It seems Melbourne's son is a…" Bella paused, trying to figure out the best way to say it so it didn't sound like she was crazy. "His son, James Melbourne, is a time traveler. So is his wife."

"Oh, so they're fairies…" Artie said, trying not to laugh at her ridiculous statement.

"What? No, I didn't say anything about wings."

"I didn't say you did. In the old days, people who showed

up confused, wearing weird clothes, speaking the same basic language but with strange accents, were called fairies. What? Haven't you been watching TV lately? It's all the rage in fiction."

"No, I don't watch TV, but I did watch old movies on VHS when I was a kid. Those were mostly musicals, though. I prefer to read books," Isabella said, her shoulders pulled back in pride.

"Who's the snob now?" Artie asked.

"Oh," her shoulders slumped. "Sorry. So, anyhow, this Marty—as he said he liked to be called—said he had grandkids born in the 18th century, somewhere around 1782. When he said his son, that's James Melbourne, liked to grow things and construct 21st century items out of 18th century materials, this Simon fellow paled. Seems like that was what he wanted to know."

"Hmm. Is there anything else?"

"He mentioned something about The Trees, but it didn't sound like he was talking about Australia. So," Isabella said, turning to face Artie, "why in the heck are you working for this creep? What does he have on you? You don't look or sound like the other numbskulls he has hanging from the rafters.

Besides, you're only half their size."

"I'd rather not say, at least not now. Just trust me, I'd rather be anywhere than in his employ. Besides, size has nothing to do with ability."

A slight blush rose on Isabella's cheeks. "As far as secrets, I don't think it will do either of us any good to have them. I know a place where we can get some passport photos taken, at least one for me. I assume you don't need to wait for getting an authentic one processed by the government," she said, a twinkle in her eye.

"Bella, today I am the government. Just let me know what name and birthdate you want to use. I can make up the rest."

***

"Don't worry about her," Phoebe told Lionel. "Izzy's an idiot. As long as she thinks I'm here against my will and that there's even the slightest chance you'll hurt me, my little sister will do whatever you want." Phoebe laughed raucously. "She was born with a severe birth defect."

When Lionel didn't act interested, she continued as if he'd asked what defect. "She was born without a spine!" She laughed again, then pulled up her skirt and sat on his lap.

"How about a lap dance before the concert gets going?"

"It's already started," he said gruffly.

"Yeah, so? I hear music, but the folks aren't drunk yet. Or at least very much. We have about an hour before their reflexes slow, but there's still enough money in their wallets to make them worth pinching. Come on, Lionel, I'm horny…" She arched her back, pressing her voluptuous chest into his face while wiggling her bottom on the crotch of his tight leather pants.

Lionel glanced at the clock. It was too late to go out to dinner and she was right about the timing for picking pockets at the concert. He'd let her tickle and tease him for twenty minutes or so, then split and pick up a burger and milkshake, making sure she was the one who was all hot and bothered and not satisfied. It might be cruel, but he loved to hear her beg for sex. There was only one thing hotter than that: when they swapped roles and he did the begging. She might be his 'sex slave,' but he was hers, too.

Chapter 3
The Fairy King

Earlier that day

The Rare Arts and Antiquities Emporium—a popular spot with tourists and grade school teachers—also housed a rare books section, seldom busy because only a few serious scholars knew of its existence. The perpetually curious and easily lost Marty Melbourne had checked the tapestry-partitioned room daily for the last two and a half months, hoping to find the mysterious curmudgeon genius, Master Simon.

He felt like such a fool now. He should have known that the short and wide, but sly and slippery, expert time traveler wouldn't be there until after the winter solstice. Whether it was superstition or not, the undeniable fact was that life grew and the thirst for knowledge blossomed after those first dormant weeks of the shortest part of the year. It was nearly the first day of the Chinese New Year and life was now awakening—the prime time to increase knowledge, to build on the foundations of the venerable sages, and to search out new secrets in the ancient tomes.

He had no reason to believe that Master Simon would be in England but the book he had used as bait had been off the library exchange list for years. Maybe it wasn't right to put the false notice in The Times that he had contributed a copy to the Rare Arts and Antiquities Emporium. Nobody at RAAE would confirm or deny the Melbourne family's contribution to their collection. Evidently, though, just the thought of it being available was enough of a lure that the insatiably curious researcher, Simon, had come out into the subterranean sea of knowledge and curiosities to investigate. And, by the presence of the six other oddly-dressed men at the corner table, Master Simon hadn't come alone.

"Would you care for a chocolate?" Marty asked, cautiously approaching the elusive and mystical fellow.

Simon glanced over at the tall, amiable man with the abundance of curly salt and pepper hair, then went back to his studies, ignoring him and his question. He had been charmed before by this wily amateur magician. He stroked the top of the ancient parchment work. It would be a very difficult sleight of hand for Martin Melbourne to make this book disappear or switch it out with another. The large, leather-bound volume with brass trimmings probably weighed five kilos. It wasn't the volume he had come to find but was a rare dissertation he had never seen and was purported to have vital information in it. Simon doubted this time-travel obsessed British lord knew Latin, much less understood the innuendos used for the secrets it contained as safeguards from the casual ancient-texts researcher. Still, he'd keep it close and not let Melbourne view it.

"Here, I have several of them," Marty said, then bit into one of the pale green-colored confections. "See, there's fancy nougat on the outside and chocolate truffle on the inside. I don't think I've ever encountered a candy so smooth yet bright. Mint chocolate as only the angels could blend..." Marty took another nibble of his candy, then set the small tin down in front of the suspicious researcher.

"Hmph," Simon remarked, then glanced up, finally acknowledging Marty. "What do you want?"

"I just wanted to bring you some of these chocolates. I remembered how much you liked them last time we met. I know I was a bit of a pest. I wanted to once again say I'm sorry."

Simon closed his eyes and breathed deeply. His upper brain said to stay away from the trickster, but his inner-child—so long ignored and repressed—said, 'Indulge me, pretty please?' He could smell the subtle scent of peppermint intermingling with the sweet, rich cocoa butter. He opened his eyes and saw that his hand had subconsciously reached for one of the confections.

"Well, all right; I guess one wouldn't hurt." He took a small bite of the chocolate and sighed at the taste that rolled all his pleasant lifetime memories into to one place and one time: the inside of his mouth.

"Go ahead—these are all for you. I think they're worthy of The Fairy King."

"Did you just call me a fairy king?" Simon asked testily, his chocolate reverie broken by the soft-spoken slight.

"Nooo," Marty replied slowly, trying to think of a way to soothe the obviously ruffled older gentleman. "I called you *The* Fairy King. I assure you, I meant no disrespect."

"I'm a master of dimensional transportation with an emphasis on acquiring rare and exotic specimens of nature and man for the benefit of furthering our understanding of life on earth," Simon replied indignantly and with one single breath. He frowned as he realized what a huge mouthful of words he had just spewed. He opened his eyes and saw Marty's shocked look coupled with an awkwardly contained grin. "I guess The Fairy King will work for you and me. But please, Lord Martin, don't introduce me to anyone as such."

"You may call me Marty," he said, and started to pat him on the shoulder. When he saw the prim and petite man straighten as only a professor with an attitude could, he changed his mind, instead grasping his other hand behind his back. "May I call you Master Simon?" Marty asked meekly.

"That would be fine. Now, what is it you need so urgently that you chose to interrupt our gathering?" Simon nodded, indicating his peers across the room. At the same time, he put his partially eaten chocolate back in the tin, surreptitiously scooting the container into the front pocket of his black frock coat.

"I'd like to know if you've seen my son, James Melbourne. He recently went 'back' to 1781. I am certain he made it from The Trees with his wife, Leah, to the Pomeroy's place. I thought there would be a record of him in the letters the Pomeroys wrote to their descendants. There was only one mention of him, then nothing more. I can't find a trace of him in *any* historical documents. He just—poof—disappeared. If he's in trouble, or was in trouble, I'd like to help him. I have a coin to travel with and know where The Trees time portal is— the same one you came through with Evie last year—but I don't know if he's anywhere near there. You do remember Evie, I'm sure. The woman you saved, but who accidentally got a biological rewind when she overdosed on the contents of one of your little blue bottles?"

"Hmph. Don't remind me. Leonardo Senior is still mad at me about that debacle," Simon said, then folded his arms and turned away, ready to be done with this Melbourne pest who always seemed to pop up at the most inopportune times.

Marty paused, trying not to be too pushy but determined to win back Master Simon's attention. "Actually, I think you may also know Benji, Evie's nephew. He's hard to miss." Marty put his hand above his head. "He's six foot seven inches tall, has bright red hair, and one of the friendliest fellows you've ever met. He went back in time from the 21st century to visit his grandfather and Aunt Evie's father-in-law, a man named Jody Pomeroy. You see, Benji was born in the 18th century, went forward to the 20th century as a child, came back to 1782 as an adult, met the lovely Janie, and then came back with her to the 21st century so they could marry. She was black, you see, an African American, and he couldn't marry her in her natal time."

Marty saw Master Simon's irritated frown that declared, 'You're rambling—get on with it,' louder than shouting through an amplified megaphone.

He winced, mumbled, "Excuse me for being so verbose," then took a deep breath and began anew. "What I'm trying to say is that when Benji came back from 1782, he told me he had seen my son, James, and his wife, Leah, and said that they now had a daughter, Bibb Elizabeth Melbourne, named after my wife. At that time, Leah had just found out she was pregnant with their second child. However, I can't find any trace of any of their histories in America. It's as if the whole family—poof—just disappeared," he repeated, using the same opened-handed gesture.

"You already said that. So, what do you expect me to do?" Master Simon asked, his chin held high, as if he was trying to pull himself up to Marty's eye level, at least.

Marty sat down in an overstuffed library chair, so Simon was now above him—literally and figuratively—and he was submitting himself to the short man's intellectual superiority.

38

"Sir, I believe you are a very talented man, and I'd like to believe you could accomplish any task you chose to undertake. Honestly, though, I have no idea how extensive your skills are. I only want to know if you could—rather would—find out about my son. Could you find out where he went, and if he was able to live a long, healthy life with his wife and children?"

Master Simon sucked in his lips and squinted his eyes in anger. He was still irritated with this man who had stolen his precious portal site map years ago and replaced it with a paper placemat from that golden arches fast food restaurant. His lips relaxed into almost a grin. Yes, he'd help the clever British citizen with the wry sense of humor. It took more than a mere commoner to pull off such a complicated switch. He respected him for his ingenuity, but even more so because he had returned the original and apologized for borrowing it without permission.

"Let me see what I can find out," Simon said. "I do remember meeting your young man a few years ago. He had just purchased a map that had been stolen from me earlier that same day. The person you know as Evie—Dani Madigan in her previous, um, existence—had rescued me from the side of the road soon after the theft. That horrid man—one of the MacLeod clan, I do believe—knocked me down, stole my purse and map, and left me for dead. Madame Madigan, a.k.a. Evie, took me to that little café where your son, young Lord James, was studying the map. I remember what he looks like, but that won't help me. Did he have any special talents or features that would make him stand out among others in the 18th century?"

"Let's see. He's bright, always tinkering—that is, creating—gadgets out of 18th century materials in order to make comfort and convenience items based on 21st century designs. And he loves to garden. He had brought with him seeds…" Marty stopped talking when he saw Master Simon's eyes widen, his once tight-featured face now slack in shock. "You know where he is, don't you?"

Master Simon looked over his shoulder at the other men in his little clique of time travelers, verifying they were still absorbed in their conversation and weren't interested in what he was up to. *They'll be fine without me for a few days, or even weeks. They're still deciding where they want to go for our annual month-long holiday. By the chuckles and back slapping, it sounds as if they're eager to visit one of the randier times and places. Leonardo Senior is sure to want to spend time in Venice, but the others are 'ooh la la-ing.' It appears Paris is their city of choice.*

Simon shuddered at the thought of the ignorant, crass, and painted women of Gay Paris of the past several centuries, then composed himself, his decision to assist the clever man in finding his son now easy to make.

"Yes, I have a general idea where he is, but I'll need your assistance. I would prefer that you accompany me on this trip. I don't mind traveling to different eras by myself, but I don't like distances, especially taking airplanes for long flights over vast oceans. Do you think you could acquire two first class tickets to Sydney on such short notice? I'd like to leave," Simon closed his eyes and concentrated on his list of tasks that needed to be done before departure. "Let's say we leave in two days. That should allow me time to take care of some unfinished business."

Marty gasped. He had told his wife he would stay home with her for at least the first year of their marriage. He exhaled slowly as he realized that Bibb was sure to forgive him, even before he asked. "Yes, I'll make the calls and find out if there are still seats available. And do I need to bring anything special?"

Master Simon looked Marty up and down. "Yes, get something a little less distinctive, maybe some woolen clothes and leather shoes. And no zippers or Velcro, please."

Marty nodded in agreement. A grin of appreciation began to appear on his face. He was going to travel back in time to see his son, but this time he had a guide. Surely he wouldn't get lost—again. However, he'd take two canteens this time, just in case.

***

"Flight QF2 boarding in five minutes," a woman's voice announced over the intercom.

Marty looked over at Simon, squirming uncomfortably in the molded plastic seat across from him. The master time traveler's hands gripped his knees, almost as if he was afraid his legs would fly up if he let go. His scowling face was soaked. Drops of water had beaded up and were now dribbling down the outside of his eyebrows, streaming over his closely-shaven cheeks, dropping off his jaws. Simon glanced over at Marty. Marty took the hint and looked away.

As soon as his traveling companion's eyes were diverted, Simon pulled a handkerchief from his vest pocket and wiped his face. The only thing worse than his sign of fear—the nervous sweat—was admitting to its presence by wiping it away in front of others.

Lord Martin Melbourne was a true gentleman, his family's hereditary status notwithstanding. Marty—as the man liked to be called—made him feel comfortable, even in tense, distasteful situations. Yes, he'd help the man, although he wasn't obligated to do so. He had been a bit melodramatic about it, but Marty had asked politely. Besides, he really didn't want to go to Paris with the others. They knew he didn't like to party, and his absence would make their festivities and carousing less constrained. He was doing them a favor and, by their lack of protests about one of their own traveling with a mere commoner, they realized it too. Now, if he could only get through the interminable flight without getting nauseous, he'd be satisfied.

Marty knew that Simon didn't like to fly—he had admitted it earlier—but he was still willing to make the trip. Whether there was an ulterior motive to the grumpy genius's decision to help him or not, it really didn't matter. Now he could find out what happened to James, Leah, and their children. And maybe talk them into returning.

Simon stayed by Marty's elbow, grateful that he had a guide. He had flown only once before, and the airplane had been much smaller than this one: only two propellers and just two seats on either side of the narrow aisle. This one had to have many more seats. The line of people waiting to board this behemoth coach snaked around the lobby, the queue partitioned off by shiny bastions threaded with heavy, wide ribbon. Nylon. Yes, that's what it was called. It was the same fabric used for those confounded seatbelts in automobiles. He shuddered. Horses may leave behind recycled clumps of hay and feed, but their odor was much less offensive than the cars and buses these twenty-first century folks were so fond of.

Simon winced, trying to control his urge to repeatedly gulp deep breaths. Now was not a good time—it never would be— to confess that he also suffered from claustrophobia. *You've been through worse, old man. You'll get through this, too. At least there weren't any bonfires in planes!*

Chapter 4
Flying

Too bad there hadn't been any first-class seats available. Marty even asked about business class, but they were sold out, too. If he had been willing to wait a week, he could have managed either class, but even then, the seats weren't together. Still, coach on an A380 airplane was plenty comfy compared to some of the flights he'd been on. As long as Simon didn't see that the front of the plane had seats that reclined into beds and were more private, the old man probably wouldn't know the difference.

Simon shuffled behind Marty down the narrow aisle, grateful that his escort patiently held up the other passengers while he got settled into the seat by the window. "I really don't need to watch the scenery," he grumbled, and pulled down the plastic window shade. He gasped with an immediate sense of claustrophobia and hastily shoved it back up. "But I do prefer natural light, after all."

"Just follow my lead," Marty said, "and you should be fine. And you need to buckle up before we take off."

Simon groaned as he reached behind his shoulder, searching for the seat belt.

"It's not like a car; this belt is actually much easier to use." Marty lifted his hip, found his own seatbelt, and held it up in illustration. "The airlines only require that you wear one of these across your lap. The chances of a head on collision are minimal, so shoulder restraint isn't required."

Marty saw Simon's face pale and break out in a fresh sweat at the same time. "If I may be so bold…" he said and reached across to point to the belt at Simon's hip.

Simon grabbed it by the metal end and held it like he was afraid it would bite him if he annoyed it, waiting for instructions on what to do with it now that he'd found it.

Marty held up his own buckle in illustration and did the oft-repeated spiel of a flight attendant. "This is how to attach and release your seatbelt." He flipped open then let the metal clasp snap shut. "Please keep it secured during the flight in case of turbulence."

Click.

He didn't think it possible, but Simon got even more pale. Marty slipped into his grandfatherly caregiver persona and explained, "Simon, flying on an airplane is safer than driving a car on the road, maybe even riding in a wagon, ahem, back in the old days. These seats can be left upright or reclined after we take off. You can nap as long as you wish, write in a journal, listen to music, watch a movie … Oh, and they even have toilet facilities in the back."

Simon looked sideways at his talkative traveling companion and sighed. Whether it took 23 minutes or 23 hours, it was going to be a long flight.

***

"I couldn't get first class seats, but that's okay since they couldn't either. They're two rows behind us. No, don't look!" Artie whispered harshly. "Trust me." He pointed to the window seat and waited in the aisle while she stepped in.

"I doubt if we could hear anything they said over the airplane noise anyhow. This way we'll be getting off before they do. We can stand back and wait to see where they go." Artie took the backpack she offered him and checked the weight of it, surprised at how light it was. "You don't have anything breakable in here, do you?"

"No. Other than the new change of clothes that you…ahem…bought me, it's just my quilt and some snacks. I didn't even remember to get toiletries."

"Don't worry about that," he said and set the bag in the overhead compartment, standing on tiptoes to make the reach. "I doubt there's anything we need that we can't buy in Sydney. I've never been there, but it's one of the major business centers in the world, catering to travelers from all continents."

"You didn't bring anything?" she asked. "Nothing at all?"

He shook his head back and forth, then changed his mind. "I brought my ID, a wallet, and," he wiggled his fingers in front of his face and grinned, "my tools. I never leave home without them."

Isabella looked around and made sure no one was listening, then leaned close to him, forcing him by her posture to bend forward to meet her. "I can't believe you're a pickpocket," she whispered.

"Why? What's a pickpocket supposed to look like?" he whispered back.

"Snarly, unshaven, desperate..."

Artie pulled back just enough that he had room to rub the side of his cheek. "I haven't had to shave in," he rolled his eyes, wanting to tell her his story, then decided against it. "I don't have much for facial hair, as you can see. Desperate?

You bet I am—or have been on more occasions than I care to share. And as far as snarly...” He lifted one side of his mouth into a sneer. “I can be snarly if I need to be.”

“Oh, shoot! Kiss me!” Bella said, and grabbed Artie by the ears and pulled him close. She pressed her rigid lips to his and watched out the corner of her eye.

Shocked, Artie froze, his fingers clenching the end of the armrest in surprise. “What?” he mumbled and tried to pull away but was met with renewed force.

What I don't do for you, dear sister. I guess this isn't as bad as what you have to endure, though. Bella relaxed into the desperate smooch, waiting for the two thugs to sit down so the kiss could be over and done with.

Artie didn't care what she had seen to make her kiss him. It'd been years since he'd enjoyed a kiss. Growing up and enduring puberty all over again had been miserable, but the late teenaged years could be fun all over again. He softened his lips, responding to hers, a sigh slipping out.

Bella resisted the urge to hum as a way to pass the time, hiding their faces in a forced kiss, then started to snicker at the thought of humming a song while kissing.

“Is it that bad?” Artie mumbled, his lips still pressed to

hers. "I can do better."

Bella pulled away and gave in to a full giggle. "I'll take your word for it." She rolled her eyes at the thought of the teenager claiming to have experience with making love, or at least making out.

Artie sighed in defeat. *Damn this youthful body! If only that little blue bottle of Fountain of Youth elixir came with instructions! How did I know that only a few drops would have cured my internal bleeding, that drinking half the bottle would rejuvenate me? At least, I didn't slip back into the diaper days. And I've finally aged to the far end of the teen years.*

"By the way," she said, emboldened by his sudden insecurity, "I kissed you so Lionel's goons wouldn't see where we were sitting. I think Lionel is making sure we don't make a fortune out of the information and leave him hanging." She groaned. "Then again, he knows I wouldn't double-cross him because he still has my sister hostage."

Be gentle with her! She obviously doesn't know. "Um, Bella, may I ask you a question?"

"You just did." Bella looked around, exasperated, then grabbed the safety placard from the seat in front of her, eager for any distraction.

Boy, is she ever stressed. She definitely doesn't know about Phoebe's infatuation with Lionel. Just ask her! "Bella, has your sister ever made a bad choice for a boyfriend?"

"Pfft! All the time. Shoot, there was this one time…" Bella looked at Artie for clues about what he was really trying to say. "Do you mean to say you think she's with Lionel because she wants to be?"

"Just saying that she sure smiles and giggles a lot for someone who's being held against her will." Artie snapped his seatbelt shut and snugged it tight. "The only time I ever saw her look even a little bit miserable was today when you came in. His other girlfriends are afraid of her. Not that he pays them any attention anymore. Phoebe's so jealous of his affections, she practically clawed one of the other girls' eyes out."

Bella groaned, remembering the reason her sister had been kicked out of school: for fighting another girl over her boyfriend's supposed infidelity. The other girl was scarred for life. "Then why did she look scared today?" *Oh, please, be a reason. I don't want to hear that I've been stealing and lying to support her and her lover!*

"Ach, what do I know. Maybe it's all my imagination. You know her, I don't. Let's just both agree that Lionel is a creep and uses people. Let's hope those two old farts give us some valuable intel so your sister can go free."

"Yeah, she can be free…" *And then where will Phoebe go, what will she do? Crap! He's probably right. Why didn't I see it before? She's got everything she wants and needs with Lionel. Why would she want to be free and on the streets? No money, no job, no home, no boyfriend. Shoot! I'm an idiot!*

"At least, we're getting a vacation to Australia," Artie said, patting her hand that still clutched the armrest. "I'll take care of you."

Bella pulled her hand away and tucked it under her other elbow. "I can take care of myself, thank you very much."

"I'm sure you can," he said, wincing at his *faux pas.* "I guess I should have said I'm sure we'll both be fine. I have a few useful skills, but I'm sure you do, too."

"You're darned right, I do," Bella said. *I just wish I knew what they were.*

Chapter 5
The Land Down Under
Welcome to Australia

"We're here," Artie whispered to Bella, sound asleep on his shoulder, a silvery thread of drool dribbling from the side of her mouth.

"Who? What? Where...I mean, did I fall asleep?" she asked and sat up straight, wiping her chin with the back of her hand, completely disoriented. She realized where she was and who she was with, then glanced down at his shoulder to make sure she hadn't slobbered on him.

"Oh, you just napped for a little bit. Like from ten minutes out of Singapore 'til now. Actually, we're still about an hour out of Sydney. The stewards brought around breakfast a few minutes ago and will be bringing around little freshen-up kits next."

"Here you are," the steward said, and handed a packet to Bella first, then to Artie. "And this, too."

"Wow! Thanks," Bella said, accepting the warm, moist washcloth. She immediately wiped her face, glad that she never wore makeup. "I thought you said they didn't have first class seats available. They're sure treating us that way."

Artie shifted positions, trying to ignore the crick in his back from not having moved for four hours, then pulled out Bella's tray. "Now that you're awake, we can eat. I had him leave our breakfasts. *Mangia!*"

"Oh, my goodness. I can't eat that much… A muffin, eggs, fruit, cereal. This is more than I eat in a week!"

Artie leaned over her shoulder and said in a husky James Cagney voice, "Stick with me, kiddo, and I'll have you eating like a queen."

A shiver ran up Bella's back at his nearness, the unexpected sensation spreading to her nipples. She looked down and saw the reaction showed through her Aladdin tee shirt and sports bra. She brought up one arm casually to brush away an invisible hair from her face, trying to cover her perky points. "Maybe you can treat this queen to a sweater. It's cold in here."

Pulling back the plastic wrap from her food tray, Artie glanced at her embarrassment, knowing that his whisper had made her jittery. *Cool! She likes me!*

"I wouldn't worry about being cold when we hit Sydney,"

he said, ignoring her blush, focused on removing all the little bits of plastic that clung to her food dish. "It may be February, but for Australians, that means it's summer. Tank tops, shorts, and sandals are the gear for this time of year. I'll set you up with a new wardrobe as soon as we find out where we're going."

Bella unwrapped her cutlery and set the napkin on her lap, ready to eat eggs for the first time in months. She stabbed a piece of omelet and stuffed the oversized bite in her mouth. "Food first, then we'll deal with whatever else comes our way."

Artie tugged the covering off his plastic tray, getting it all off at once. "Works for me!" he said, biting off the word 'darlin'. *And I thought Lionel was being a jerk, sending me off with phony Phoebe's little sister. She's a treat!*

***

"Don't leave my side," Artie said when they finally emerged from the long customs queue. "I've been watching the goons. I doubt that they're armed, but they're Lionel's old sparring partners. They're not championship material, but they get their jollies by inflicting pain on anyone smaller than they are."

"Oh, no," Bella said, then snuggled close to him to avoid being crushed by a large woman coming down the aisle. "By the way you groaned when you said that, it sounds as if you were on the other end of their enjoyment."

"I did not groan," he said, "but yes, I did suffer…a time or three."

"I was joking!" Bella hissed, then put her head on his shoulder and rubbed it back and forth affectionately. "Am I supposed to be extra friendly to you or not?"

"Kiss me," he said and pulled her into the alcove next to the phone-charging station.

"Why?" Bella asked, and pulled away from him.

"Okay. You could have just got us both killed. It was a test, all right? You need to do as I tell you, right away, no questions asked. I'm serious when I say your life could depend on it."

"My life? Or yours?"

"Most likely, both. What difference does it make? You're so hot and bothered about saving your dumb sister that you don't even take care of yourself. Right now, I need your help and you could care less. All you care about is *Phoebe*," he said, mocking her name. "How do you think that makes me feel? If I don't get that information for Lionel, he'll kill me."

"Wait. What are you talking about?" Bella hissed in a loud whisper. She looked around, making sure no one was interested in their confrontation, then started again. "Your own brother would kill you? Are you sure? And why are you saying, 'my dumb sister'? And how am I not taking care of myself? You seem to know all about me, but you don't know shit!"

Artie looked up, focused on something behind Bella, and said, "Kiss me."

Bella groaned, changing the tone from exasperated to enamored in the middle of the guttural moan, then kissed him, a full, open-mouthed, tongue-tickling kiss that she should have saved for the man she would marry, but what-the-hell?

Artie succumbed to her passionate kiss—both arms wrapped around her as if she would fall through the cracks in the tile if he let go—then remembered to keep one eye open. Master Simon and that Melbourne fellow were heading to the curb, followed by the goons. Bella's tongue probed deeper into his mouth, causing his one opened eye to shut and his lower body parts to burgeon. *Hell! Stand up and follow them!*

Wake up, man! "Bella…"

"Yeah?" she answered dreamily.

"We have to follow them…" Artie bent forward, picked up Bella's backpack and held it in front of his bulging fly. "I'll take this. Just grab my arm. Oh, and by the way, if anyone asks, we're newlyweds."

Bella's smile literally hurt her cheeks. She licked her bottom lip and let the smile grow even bigger. "Works for me, dear," she said, and grabbed his arm, snuggling close. "And if I get cold, I know where to go to get warm."

I don't know what I've got myself into, but I think I like it! Shoot, as crazy as it seems, I might even love it!

***

"Why did you kiss me?" Bella asked, her sated smile now morphed into a slight frown of curiosity.

"Well, one reason was those goons were looking all over the place for me, trying to see if I was watching them follow Simon and Melbourne. It worked—they didn't see my face. They may be powerful punchers, but they can't fake not seeing me."

Still feeling the powerful effect of their shared passionate kiss, Artie braved a sweet simple buss on Bella's pouty lips.

"Don't be disappointed, darlin'. The kiss worked. Plus, you did as I asked and didn't question me. That immediate reaction wasn't for a life or death situation, but it could possibly have had a painful ending. I don't think their presence is sanctioned."

"Huh?"

"I don't think those goons are here because Lionel sent them. I think they're freelancing. They want whatever it is that these Fairies are after."

"Fairies? Oh, yeah. The time travelers."

"Stay here a minute. Keep an eye on Simon and Melbourne. It looks like they're waiting for a shuttle. I'll be right back." Artie looked towards the men's restrooms and gave her a weak smile of embarrassment and a shoulder shrug.

"All right. I'll claim a table, preferably a stand up one with a view." She rubbed her fanny. "I'm not too eager to sit down again, at least not for a few more hours."

"Okay. I'll be right back." He leaned forward, ready to touch his forehead to hers, then decided the gesture was too flirtatious for someone who looked so young. *I wish I'd hurry up and hit another growth spurt. At least I'm better off than I was three years ago when I struggled through my second adolescence, complete with acne and squeaky voice.*

"Oh, excuse me, sir," Artie said as he bumped into the portly traveler, the two of them rushing through the doorway to the restroom at the same time.

"No worries," the man said, then hurried to the urinal as Artie made his way into a stall.

Artie locked the door, then reached into his jacket and pulled out the wallet he had lifted. *Cool! Cash. Good ol' Australian greenbacks and more! This ought to keep us fed and housed for at least a week.* He returned a couple fivers and the ID back in the wallet, held it by the edges and wiped it down with toilet paper to get his prints off, then casually dropped it behind the toilet. Someone was bound to find it. No use taking charge cards that could be traced. Besides, because there was still money in it, when it was eventually found, it would appear as if it fell out of the man's pocket and theft wouldn't be suspected. Unless the guy who found it ripped him off. By the cut of the big man's suit, he had plenty more where these bucks came from.

Artie tapped his other pocket, verifying his other prize was still there. He'd check out the phone later. Right now, he'd better scram before his target realized he was missing a couple valuables.

Walking up on Bella's blind side, Artie resisted the urge to pat her round bottom, but did succumb to giving her a peck on her flawless and unpainted cheek. "Hello again, my newlywed wife."

Bella rolled her eyes in apparent frustration at her role but couldn't stifle a blush of excitement, recalling their ground-shaking, heart-thumping kiss. *Will we have to share the same room? Of course. The same bed? Probably. Will he want to…*

"Hey, knucklehead. Wake up. You're off in your own little world again. Looks like Simon and Melbourne are still waiting for their shuttle. Hand me one of those powdered coffee creamers, would you?"

"Why? You don't have any coffee."

Artie leaned close, tapping his forehead to hers, this time for another lesson in cooperation. "What did I say about doing what I asked without question? If you don't trust me, we're doomed."

Foreheads still touching, Bella pushed towards him, asserting independence without claiming dominance. "I didn't think handing over coffee creamer was covered under the topic of life or death situations."

"You never know who or what will make that difference. Now, powdered coffee creamer, please."

Bella pulled away, the loss of physical contact slightly depressing, and held up two packets. "One or two?"

"One should do it, but you never know." Artie took both and set them down, then pulled out the stylish smartphone he had lifted. The first thing he did was pull off the colorful case and hand it to Bella. "Would you please dispose of this. Discreetly."

Bella took the neon orange case, wrapped it up with a fistful of napkins from the dispenser, then, just to make sure it didn't look suspicious, grabbed a leftover sandwich wrapper from the next table and folded it around the bundle so it looked like she was tossing away the rest of her sandwich. She felt Artie's eyes on her as she walked to the other side of the dining area to dispose of it.

"I thought it might be a good idea to have it far away from us," she said when she came back, "just in case. You never know when or where it's going to be a life or death situation."

Artie acknowledged her comment with a grunt. *Thank God*

the voice change is finally over. She certainly wouldn't be turned on with a squeaky voice! Good grief! Turned on? What are you thinking…

"Ahem. Looks like I'm not the only one who travels off into another world. So, once again, what are you doing?"

A blush rose on Artie's cheeks. *Caught again in a fantasy. Looks like he'd volunteer to tote her backpack…once again in front of his bulging fly, not on his back.*

"I'm disclosing body oils," he said. "This phone has both a haptic touch pattern and a fingerprint ID. I think if I get the pattern right before three tries, the print ID won't be needed. Or I hope that's the case. It all depends on how he set it up."

Bent over, intent on the task before him, Artie sprinkled the powdered creamer on the phone's screen, blew it off gently, and saw a distinct 'L' pattern. Now all he had to do was guess where to start. *Maybe he's clever and starts at the right and brings it left and up. Nope. Dang! Okay, one more try…*

"Kiss me," Bella said, and grabbed his face and pulled him away from his code-cracking.

"Wha…" Artie started to protest, but she was insistent, her hands on his ears, clutching him to bring his lips to hers. *I hope she knows what she's doing… Oh, who cares.* He relaxed into her unemotional kiss, trying to find some passion in their lip contact, but there wasn't any. *I'll show you.*

Teenaged hormones and emotional reflexes took over, Artie's decrypting of the smartphone's lockout mechanism forgotten as he turned to face Bella and gave in to his long-denied urge to grab her fanny and pull her towards him. *Ummm…*

Bella used all her upper brain power to keep one eye opened, focused on her subject, as Artie suddenly turned into a passion monster, one hand clutching her bottom close to him, the other in the middle of her back, his mouth on hers, desperate to make his one with hers. *Gotta keep watching that vampire… Don't close that eye…*

"Good morning, Bella. I hope the time difference wasn't a problem for you," Cleveland said, the smile on his face an echo of the chuckle in his voice.

Huh? Bella brought one arm up and pushed Artie away and used the other one to wipe his moist kiss away. "Cleveland? Wha…what are you doing here? *And how did you get from the front entrance to here in a millisecond?*

"I was traveling with my friends and saw you and this

young man, shall we say, interacting. I'm curious—is he friend or foe?"

"I...I...I'm her husband," Artie said, then made the same kiss-erasing gesture Bella had used to wipe his own face.

"You don't sound too sure about that," Cleveland said. "Are you sure?"

Bella moved in close to Artie and threaded her arm into the crook of his elbow. "I'm sure. We're newlyweds."

"There he is," the chubby businessman said, pointing out Artie to the police officer next to him. "He's the one who picked my pocket."

Cleveland walked forward toward the excitable man and his official escort and asked, "Is there a problem, officer?"

The security agent looked sideways at the red-faced gentleman, now in front of Artie, shaking his finger at him. "I know it was you!" he screamed, bits of spittle flying out in a two-foot radius from his mouth. "You bumped into me and stole my phone and my wallet!"

Suddenly, Cleveland was in between the angry businessman and Artie. "Normally, I'd say this was a matter for the authorities, but as a friend of this young man, I'd like to know if you have any proof. Merely existing in the same close proximity to a person does not mean he is a thief. If that were the case, who's to say that you didn't steal from him?"

"Me? Steal from that little punk? Don't be ridiculous!"

"If you don't mind, officer, can we take this to a more discreet area?"

Both intimidated and mesmerized by Cleveland's bodybuilder size and model good looks, the officer nodded. "Yes, I think that's a good idea." He gently touched the fat businessman's elbow, urging him to the security office.

"Get your hands off me!" he screeched and turned in the direction of the office. "I've never been so insulted in my life!"

"Who's your friend?" Artie whispered to Bella as they walked to the brightly-lit security area.

Still arm-in-arm, she pulled him close and answered, "I can't tell you. But I think he's one of the good guys."

"Let's hope so. I'd hate the bad guys to be that size."

"If you'd come in here, young man," the uniformed man behind the security counter asked.

Artie let go of Bella's arm and moved to the back of the small room, hoping the ordeal wouldn't get too intense. *Keep the aura of innocence. If worse comes to worst, you can always claim that hothead planted his phone on you.*

"Excuse me, but I have to frisk you. This man insists you stole his wallet and his phone," the agent said.

"Go for it," Artie said. "But I have to tell you, this is a lousy way to start my honeymoon."

The frisker gave a more thorough exam than necessary, certain that the baby-faced youth was the thief. "He's clean, sergeant. Now, would you bring the other man in?"

"I've never been so insulted…"

"That's what you said before." The agent patted down the businessman's sides and stopped when he came to the first bulge in his jacket pocket. "What's this?" he asked and opened it up. "This is a passport, but it isn't yours. This belongs to the young man!"

He patted the other side and pulled out the smartphone, sans the neon orange cover. "Is this your phone?"

"No! I mean, I don't think so. Mine had a cover on it. And I don't know how his passport got in my pocket. He must have planted it."

The agent gave the phone to the sergeant. He turned it over and saw it was like his own. He held onto the edges and presented it to the accuser, face up. "Sir, this phone has a fingerprint recognition security device. Would you put your thumb here, please?"

"Why I never…" he huffed, then set his jaw forward, sure that this scenario would end with his integrity returned, despite the passport that had mysteriously appeared on his person.

Hello, Thomas…

"Sounds like this phone likes your print. Shoot, she even said hello to you." The sergeant handed back the phone.

"Sir," the agent said, "I think this is the wallet he's looking for. At least, the photo ID looks like him. Someone found it in one of the stalls in the bathroom a few minutes ago and returned it."

"Does this look like your wallet, sir." The sergeant held it up, then opened it up. "Thomas Thomasson, is it?"

The businessman now known to be Thomas Thomasson opened the wallet, thumbed through his charge cards to verify none were missing, then opened the other section and saw his fat wad of hundred-dollar bills was missing. "I've been robbed! I had over twenty-five hundred dollars in here an hour ago, and now all I have is," he pulled out the bills and counted them, "thirty-five dollars!"

"Even if there was a way to prove you had that much money in cash," Cleveland said, "who's to say you didn't just spend it on some trinket." He nodded to the fat diamond pinkie ring Thomas sported. "Money comes and goes so quickly."

Thomas looked up at Cleveland and glared, not wanting to argue with someone not in a position of authority. Instead, he turned back to the sergeant. "Whoever turned in the wallet had to be the thief!"

The agent at the desk snorted and laughed, then composed himself and said, "It was Father O'Reilly. If he was the one who took your money, I'm sure he'll put it to good use. He runs the orphanage at the edge of town."

"If you're done with my friends, Sergeant, would you return young Artie's passport?" Cleveland asked, then looked toward the outdoor exit. "He has a shuttle to catch."

"It's in his backpack!" Thomas exclaimed, wound up all over again. "I'm sure it is! Either the money or my phone is in there!"

"You already have your phone," the sergeant said, "and any money in his bag is his. I don't have any reason to search it."

Artie unzipped the backpack, looked inside, and donned his poker face. He held up a new-to-him smartphone and two envelopes. "Just our phone and our," he looked into the first envelope, "hotel reservations," he quickly glanced into the other one that held tickets of some sort and either gift cards or credit cards, "and a few wedding gifts. I assure you, Mr. Thomasson, nothing in here is yours."

The agent answered his phone and listened to the distressed caller while Artie gave his explanation to the others.

"All right. We'll send someone right over." He turned to the sergeant. "Lou, there's some sort of kerfuffle over in the video games area. I guess there's an Elvis impersonator who's decided to give a free karaoke show. People are going nuts over there. Some are saying he's the real deal."

"Ah, yes, the Elvis impersonators convention," Bella said, ready to assist Cleveland in his clever diversion and thank him for his surprise dowry. "My husband and I will be attending the event tonight. He's a contestant, you know. The best Elvis in Liverpool! Show them, sweetheart."

This must be her version of Kiss Me. Artie put his head down dramatically, handed Bella the backpack without looking at her, took a deep breath, then looked up and snarled his upper lip. He rotated a few quick and vibrant hip shakes and shimmies, then said, "Thank you, thank you very much."

"Not bad," the sergeant said, and handed him his passport. "You're free to go, but please, don't give any free concerts here. I think we have enough to handle as it is."

Cleveland ushered the young couple out of the security office and toward the exit. "If you would," he nodded to the blue and red shuttle ahead of them, the driver all elbows as he searched under the hood for why it wouldn't run. "I think you'll find what you need at Blackheath," he added in a soft voice.

"But, but..."

Bella's protest was cut off by Artie. "I think I have the shuttle tickets in here, right, sir? Thanks for the assist. If *you* need anything, just let us know."

"Indeed, I will," Cleveland said, then turned to leave the pair, gliding his long fingers over the trim on the side of the shuttle van as he walked passed it, the motor roaring to life at his touch."

"Well, I'll be..." Artie said.

"I certainly hope you're not..." Bella replied under her breath. *One vampire in my life is enough!*

Cleveland walked away, smiling.

Bella and Artie's search for the Fountain of Youth elixir had unintentionally involved Marty and Simon and therefore ensured the Möbius factor and the timeline had not—would not—be skewed, folded, or torn in two. Simon would make sure James remained in the 18th century. Cleveland looked at the city names on the arrival and departure billboard. They were as they should be. Melbourne was still Melbourne and not Caesar City. The Melbourne Legacy had already been resolved.

He would have had it under control with his own crew but had forgotten what a showoff Elvis was when he had a potential audience. The man loved to perform. His spontaneous exhibition caused him to miss his ride. He'd never engage him again for a mission without Mark Twain. The older Southern gentleman would be needed to rein in the younger one for quite a few more years.

As it turned out, this little minx of a spy Bella was just the right one to slip into Simon's realm. If she could take his last vial of Fountain of Youth elixir, it would be safe from other hands until he could get it back from her. This clever young pickpocket, Artie, wasn't who he seemed to be, either. He was wise beyond his apparent years...

And that's when Cleveland realized that he had been duped. He grinned. No harm done. If all went well, the young lass would get what she wanted with an affectionate young man as a bonus. He hadn't noticed it at first, but now he was certain—Artie had imbibed Fountain of Youth water at least once in his life. He was definitely an older soul and from his youthful looks, knew exactly what he was looking for. He chuckled. Even if he didn't know how to dose properly.

And Bella. She looked like Kat, his dear first and only love, but she was much purer of heart. Plus, she had a lot more spunk. Now that she had a partner, he noticed a change in her aroma. Whether she knew it yet or not, her spirit had claimed the rejuvenated Artie. The young couple had the potential for a long, enjoyable life. Especially if the fast-fingered thief got his hands on Simon's little blue bottle of elixir.

***

Bella and Artie dashed to the shuttle. "Sorry we're late," Artie said, the tickets Cleveland had provided in hand. "We were detained by security." He stepped up to the side of the little stepstool in front of the van door and held Bella's hand as she readied to get on.

"Sorry, you two," the driver said, wiping the grease from his hands with a blue paper towel. "We're full. You'll have to wait for the next one."

"We have plenty of room," Marty Melbourne called out from inside the van. "It doesn't look like those two will be coming back. At least, I hope they don't. I sure wouldn't want to catch what they have."

Bella and Artie looked back where he was pointing. Lionel's two bloated freelancing goons who were searching for the same little blue bottle of Fountain of Youth water were bent over opposite ends of a concrete planter, puking into the bed of pink and purple petunias. Bella looked back for her tall benefactor and saw Cleveland watching her, his arms crossed over his chest, a smile of satisfaction making his already spectacular good looks even more stunning.

"Hmm. Bad tacos, probably. So, we're cool then?" Artie asked, attempting once again to hand the driver the tickets, this time with a tenna sitting on top.

"Absolutely! Climb on in," he said and took the bundle,

checking and returning the tickets but keeping the cash. "Next stop, the Blue Mountains."

"Why don't you take that seat, Artie, so you can lie down? I'll sit back here with these gentlemen."

Bella didn't wait for his answer but moved to the back and sat between the two fairies: Marty Melbourne—the man who had been searching for information about his lost son—and Master Simon, the grumpy short man in the vintage frock coat who seemed to be suffering from chronic dyspepsia.

Artie stifled a yawn with his hand, then set the backpack on the window side of the seat. "I think I'll take you up on your offer," he said, then snuggled his face into the pack, his knees tucked up so most of him fit, his ankles dangling over the two-person bench. One more yawn, and he was out. His last thought was that thirty-six hours without sleep is a long time for anyone, young or old.

"Is he your younger brother?" Marty asked.

Bella giggled and shook her head. "We're newlyweds. We just flew in from London. It's been a long flight. I slept part of the way, but I don't think he did. Are you going to Blackheath, too?"

Simon, absorbed in his own thoughts, had ignored the

curly-haired waif when she got on but now sat up straighter, curious about why she'd want to talk about Blackheath. It wasn't on the itinerary although it was near their destination.

Ignoring the other man's sudden change in posture and attitude, Bella continued her conversation with Marty Melbourne. The affable older man was almost identical to the dream dad she had fantasized when she was younger. She had never known hers but would enjoy this man's presence today as a special treat to herself.

"Yes, we're going there to look for my son." Marty felt the burning glare of Simon but ignored it. "I haven't seen him in a while and last I heard, he was in the area."

"If he's as good looking as you, he'll be easy to spot." Bella swallowed her gasp. "I'm sorry. That was a bit forward. It's just that you don't look or sound like a local, at least the ones I saw at the airport. I mean…" She huffed in frustration. "I did get *some* sleep on the plane, but it didn't take care of my idiot mouth syndrome."

"No worries. Yes, he does look quite a bit like me. Of course, his hair is all pepper, no salt." Marty reached up and touched his silver-haired temple and winked. "Here, take my card. If you hear or see him, please let me know. I guess I should have printed up some photos. Oh, wait, I have a picture on my phone."

Marty swiped the screen and opened the photo folder, then searched until he found it: the first, last and only picture ever taken of his entire family. He held it up to Bella and winced, remembering his wife's face was all purple and swollen. "That's my wife, his mother. We were still at the hospital. She was recovering from… Anyhow, that's my older son Billy, and that one's James Melbourne, the son I'm looking for, and his wife, Leah."

Bingo! James is the name of the one I'm supposed to make sure stays in the 18th century. Crap! I don't know anything about this fairy, time-traveling stuff. I wish I could ask Artie about it. Man, he looks sexy.

"He's sleeping soundly," Marty said, noticing her longing look. "Newlyweds, you say?"

Inhaling deeply, hoping she didn't sound as eager as she suddenly felt, Bella said, "Very newly."

Simon suddenly shifted nervously in his seat and turned to Bella. "Did you say you two were from London, and that young man is called Artie?"

"Actually, he's from Liverpool. His name is Arthur and he

calls himself Artie. I guess his original nickname was Wort, but his brother morphed that into Worthless. He didn't like that name, and I wouldn't either." Bella's face pinched into anger, recalling Lionel's pudgy hand, squeezing her sister's breast in dominance, claiming her as his personal entertainment until she could bring him his precious little blue bottle. Hopefully, one of these men had it.

"Are you all right?" Marty asked. "When you mentioned Artie's brother, you looked like you wanted to bite the man's face off."

"I'd rather use a cricket bat to smash it in," she said, then realized how violent she sounded. "I'm sorry. I shouldn't have said that, even if it is the truth. I probably wouldn't have the nerve to do it, anyhow, since he's now my," Bella shuddered in realization, "my brother-in-law." *Now that's a disgusting thought. At least, it's only make-believe.*

Simon fumbled at his side, unbuckled his seatbelt, and stood up. "Driver, driver!" he said, waving his arms to get his attention.

Marty leaned across Bella. "What's wrong, Simon?" he whispered. "We'll be there soon. It's only an hour to Blackheath and this van's a lot faster than being on a horse or in a carriage!"

"It's not the conveyance," Simon snapped back. He glanced at Bella, stretched tall and pressed back into her seat so the two men could have their discussion without being in her face. "It's something I'd rather not discuss in front of the young lady."

"Don't mind me," Bella said, and brought her elbows up so she could stick her fingers in her ears. "Go for it." *Yes, please do explain. My fingers won't go deep. You didn't get excited until I said Artie was given the nickname Worthless by his brother. I want to know why.*

Simon looked back at the young girl, her face expressionless, eyes forward, fingers beneath her curly hair, plugging off sound with her long slender fingers. He sat back down and focused on Marty. "I thought that young man looked familiar. However, when I saw him last, he was much older and ill. He pinched my bottle of elixir, right out of my inner coat pocket. In his defense, he did look like he had one foot in a coffin—and too weak to pull the other one in—when he nicked it. I'm sure he drank it—probably saved his life, although it looks like he imbibed too much. The man's brother, Lionel the Loanshark, is a notorious manipulator in

Liverpool. He controls the gambling, unlicensed liquors, and the services of, shall we say, amenable consorts of both genders."

"But why do we have to get off the shuttle? I want to go back and see James, and you said Blackheath is where our time portal is."

"Lord Martin, your thinking is so constrained. Australia is ripe with portals. The closest one to the First Settlement site—where we should find your son—is just outside of Paramatta. It's a bit difficult to find, and we'll have to hire a driver, but that's what I've decided we're going to do." Simon sat back, arms folded. No further discussion needed nor desired.

Marty reached across Bella and tapped Simon on the shoulder. "But why the change?"

Simon looked at Bella to make sure she wasn't listening. By her frozen stare straight ahead, she was just a moment or two away from falling asleep sitting up, and it was still safe to speak. "Because I don't trust him," he hissed.

"All right. If you're sure the other site will be a better option," he sighed in defeat, "I'll follow without argument."

Chapter 6
The Legend
of Three Giants

Scotland
November 14, 2014

Becky MacKay-Melbourne has just been rescued by her husband, Australian-born Jim Melbourne, and her brother and fellow time-traveler, Benji MacKay, using clues given in a letter written by 20th century-born James Melbourne over two hundred years earlier. Jim never believed in Fairies—real everyday people who traveled through time—but the letter might make him change his mind.

***

'The Letter'

"Dear All,

"If Becky was taken by those dastardly MacLeod males (they're not worthy of being called men), and Jim and Benji immediately went to Swona Island, then all should/will be fine. If this box wasn't opened on receipt, or if the instructions in these letters were ignored and the name Jim Melbourne means nothing to the reader, then my condolences or I'm sorry; the following is just the ramblings of a malnourished and lonely convict.

"But, if Jim Melbourne is reading this, then he listened and answered my wish for him to come back to save me. If he hadn't, he wouldn't be alive nor would any of his ancestors, at least for six generations back.

"You see, Jim, the first time you read this, you are a disbeliever. You don't believe—haven't believed—your wife and her family about time travel, even though it really does exist and they've all experienced it firsthand.

"And for the MacKays: I have discovered that you have control over which year you 'pop into,' as it were. In other words, it isn't just a fixed two hundred years or so that you can go back or forward. As long as you have a focus—a person you can concentrate on in the time period you're going to—can find the right portal, and have the coin, then you can travel. I only mention this because I need you to come help me in 1789 Australia.

"Actually, if you are Jim Melbourne and reading this, you already have/will come back. Benji and Janie are going to try to get you to come with them, but you are/were a hard sell.

The first letter I wrote—the 'read me first' letter—was in my own blood. At the time, that was all I had for ink. Rather than rewrite it, I left it as it was. The direness of my circumstances led me to use blood, but now I realize that you, as a cop, can scrape a sample of it and verify who I am. My grandfather kept a baby album for me. There is a lock of hair in it that you can use as a DNA sample for verification. I'm not sure if the modern tests can carbon date or whatever the blood sample to verify that it is over 200 years old, but I hope so. If not, you'll just have to have faith like the rest of us did.

"I was recently blessed with paper, ink, and quill, so I will make the best of it and let my story be known.

"Last month I was saved from certain death by The Three Giants. There is an old Aboriginal legend about three very large people who came from the underworld to show 'the people' the way to their new leader. The queen was the tallest black woman anyone had ever seen. She was served by two white men who were even taller than her. One of them had dark hair and the other—his hair the color of fire—called himself her consort. The three had come to tell 'the people' of their new leader, a special white man who would keep the evil white men from taking over their land.

"Well, do I need to tell you that Janie was the queen, Benji her consort, Jim her warrior general, and I'm now their new advisor? The nice aspect of time travel is that I have years, maybe even decades, to write to you and ask you to join me, to save me from certain death at the gallows. You already have, but I still need to put pen to paper and ask you to do it. Then I'll need to find a way to send the letter to you in the 21st century. So, since nothing is certain, I have decided to send you the information write away. Pardon the pun; I guess I'm missing my dear sweet mother-in-law, Evie Pomeroy-Hart, more than I thought.

"Jim, when you were here, you told me that my wife and my first three children would be here in a year or so. I'll just have to make sure I take care of myself and try not to lose any more teeth before they get here. I'd hate to scare my children with my new, gapped-tooth smile. I'd like to say the other guy looked worse than I did after the row, but he was already quite ugly. I, on the other hand, now look like a seasoned hockey player without my two front teeth.

"What I need is for you, Jim—or even my brother, Billy—to put together a picture of me with my new features so you'll have a focus point for travel. I'm sure the police departments have programs even better and more accurate than police sketch artists. Bibb—that is Bibb the first, my mother—should still have a copy of the family picture we had taken before I came back to 1781 North Carolina. You can use that as a baseline photo. From there, please deduct at least 40 pounds. I'm not sure what I weigh now, but I used to be six foot even and weigh 175 pounds. I suppose I'm the same height, but months of near starvation and dysentery has taken its toll. I have a two-inch scar above my left eyebrow. It bisects the brow midway and at a two o'clock angle as viewed from in front of me. My teeth were already getting loose from scurvy, although I have been diligent in eating every green weed I can find, save the eucalyptus. I don't know how the koalas do it. I tried, but I guess I have the wrong kind of stomach.

"But I digress and am wasting time, paper, and ink. Fights are common around here, and that's how I lost my two front teeth. Rum is a precious and much sought after commodity and most of the rows are about it or loose women. Actually, the women don't have much choice, and I thank the Lord that I'm not one. I know from my schooling that the next few years will be easier on the women who arrive later, especially the ones who aren't prisoners. When you told me that it wouldn't be for a while before Leah and the children would join me, I was heartbroken that I'd have to wait, but happy that they were coming.

"According to you, my father, Marty Melbourne, found another magnetic portal just north of Paramatta. I have tried to get there, but the governor isn't exploring that region. Yet. I'm working on it, though.

"Hopefully, Marty has been able to return with the map. I forgot to ask you if he had it when you were here, and I know I haven't seen him since I first arrived in North Carolina in 1781. His crummy sense of direction seems to include his finding the right time along with the right place.

"I'm out of room. More later.

Love,

James Melbourne

Christmas 1788

***

"Becky, if you think you and the kids will be all right, I'd like to go back to Sydney for a few days. That is, if Benji and

Janie will come with me. For this…ahem…venture, I think I'll need them as guides."

Benji shook his head in confusion. "What do ye mean, Jim? Janie and I have never been to the land down under. How could we be your guides? You were the one born there."

Becky sidled up to Jim and wrapped her arms around his waist. "The children and I will be fine. Mom and Da wanted to stay a few more days, anyhow. But why do you want to go back to Australia? I thought you had some mysterious reason for staying away," Becky asked, her grimace of frustration barely contained.

"I ken I told ye I never wanted to go back, but this is for my great-granddad. He did ask in the letter that I come and visit. And well, I want to get it done as soon as possible. I mean, I dinna think I'll forget to go back, but I have this itchy, crawly feeling that now is better than later. Plus, your newlywed brother and his wife were wantin' to go back home to America. I thought that I'd be better off if the three of us went together now, before it was time for them to return. I know how to schedule a flight to Sydney, and I can find my way to the first settlement with just about any map, but…um…I'll need someone to show me how to get to the right time."

"Janie, would you like to go to Australia to see James again?" Benji asked. "Ye did seem to get along well with him when we were back in 1783 North Carolina."

Jane nodded. "I'd like to see everyone again, but I don't think that can happen. I'd still be considered a slave if we returned, not your wife. Now, how far away is this Australia?"

Just then, four-year-old Bibby popped up at Uncle Benji's elbow with her own papier-mâché and poster paint version of the earth. "We're right here," she said, pointing to the bright yellow smear that represented Scotland. "And you were born somewhere in Africa, right? That's this big red continent. I was waiting until we found out where you were born so I could make it a prettier color, too." Bibby turned the wrinkly globe to the other side. "And here is Australia, where my daddy and a lot of my other kin were born. They call it 'the land down under' because it's on the underside of the world. At least it is if you're up here in the northern hemisphere. And hemisphere just means half globe or half round thing. A basketball's a sphere, too. Over on this side of Australia is Sydney, the greatest harbor in the world! That's where the First Fleet landed. Well, sort of. It wasn't a town then, but it did have a lot of water, more than enough for the eleven ships that sailed into it, huh, Daddy?"

"And there's your geography and history lesson all at the same time, Janie," Jim said.

Benji looked to his young niece. "Thank you, Bibby." He turned to Janie and took her hand. "Now, I've got our passports. Are ye ready fer another adventure, my dear wife?"

Jim bit his bottom lip as he looked at Jane, hoping she was willing to go on yet another long flight.

"Let's see. I've got good company whether I stay here or go. But if we all go, we'll be helping James... No question in my mind. I'm ready when you are, but we may have to change our return tickets to America. I want to make up lost time with everyone here. My new family. I never thought I'd have one this big or wonderful."

***

Remote area of New South Wales, Australia
Three days later

"Are ye sure we're in the right place, Jim? It doesna look like anyone has been here before. Ever!" Benji said, trying to hold back his exasperation. An interminable flight, a rental

89

car that was too small for the three of them, and now this.

"Weel, I ken this is just above the place I used to play when I was a lad. There was a spot down that beach," Jim said, pointing to a barren jetty, "where we'd find one of the locals, give him a few bucks over the cost, and he'd get us a case of beer. It'd last us all night. Of course, my mates would pass out after jest a few, and then I'd have the rest fer myself. But I canna see the bar or the beach house from here. Everythin' else looks the same, though. I mean, are ye sure we already went back?" he asked, suddenly very insecure at his old stomping grounds.

"Ach, so now ye believe, aye?" Benji asked, a smile in his voice as he gave his new friend and brother-in-law's back a hearty thump.

Jim blushed, then admitted reluctantly, "Ye did tell me that I'd get the queasy stomach and aye, I believe ye now. But, I'm sorry. I...I must not have concentrated like I was supposed to. I mean, I was a bit leery of the whole scheme. What I'm tryin' to say is, I'm not sure if we're in the right place, I mean the right time. I jest imagined this place without anyone here, pristine and without any beer cans or bars or...or...I'm sorry. I think we're too early, maybe a few centuries too early even. And I dinna concentrate on the picture of the other Jim Melbourne, either."

"Weel, the day is young, the bartender is still at the bar, and if we can all concentrate on him, we can go back and try it again. I dinna ken if we can go from here to James without goin' back to the 21st century first, though..." Now Benji was insecure and scared but didn't want to share his uneasiness with the other two.

"Why not?" Jane asked.

"Weel...I...um... Gee, I guess we can try," Benji replied.

"I think maybe we should wait a bit, though," Jim said hesitantly. "I think we have company."

Benji and Jane turned around and looked to where Jim was staring. Four small Bushmen, totally naked—each with a spear in one hand, the other covering his loins—were staring at them.

"Go na inyanook," Jim said in greeting.

"Go na tungooja," the man standing slightly in front of the other three replied with a big grin.

"Let me do the talking," Jim said softly to his two companions. "I ken a bit of the lingo, but I dinna ken when we are or if the dialect is the same now as when I was a lad."

The apparent leader walked up to Jim and poked him softly just below the belly with his stick. "Go na inyanook?" He repeated Jim's declaration, but as a question, snorted, then looked up to see Jim's response.

"What did ye say to him?" Benji asked under his breath.

"I thought I said, 'Good day to you,'" Jim replied without looking at him, a pleasant smile pasted on his face as he gently nodded to the small, dark man who still had his hunting stick poked into his privates.

"Go na tungooja!" the leader crowed, then nodded to his hand, full of man parts, and puffed his chest in pride.

"Oh, shit," Jim said and gulped. He shook his head and said, "No, no, no, no!"

The four Aborigines began laughing and pointing at Jim's crotch, shaking their heads like Jim had, making clicking noises that evidently meant something.

"Did ye jest say ye had wee man parts?" Benji asked.

"Um, I think so," Jim answered. "I'm going to kick Charlie's butt next time I see him. He told me that go na inyanook banta bootu meant 'good day to you'. I think it means I have a little dick. Sorry, Janie, for being so crude."

"Well, that's better than saying that you didn't have one at all. Here, let me try," she said, then walked over to the obvious leader. The others had backed away as soon as she spoke. She had noticed their amazement at her size and voice and was going to make use of their awe.

"Hello, sirs. I am the great big queen and these are my men. He is my husband," Jane said. She put her arm through Benji's, held him close, and smiled at him. "And he is my general, my guardian." She looked at Jim and narrowed her eyes, telling him wordlessly to act the part.

Jim sucked in a deep breath, took two determined steps forward to stand in front of Jane and Benji, and placed his knuckles on his hips in a Mr. Clean power stance.

"I think this is where ye tell them that yer gonna send them a protector. I mean, that James will come and be their advocate," Benji whispered to her.

"I will send you a small big man," Jane said to her rapt audience. She pointed to Jim, then moved her hands together to indicate a smaller version of him. "James Melbourne," she said, then made the same hand movement. She walked over to Jim and whispered, "Open your mouth."

Jim opened his mouth slightly. Jane nudged up his upper lip and placed the first joint of her index finger over his two front teeth. "James Melbourne," she reiterated. She then made a slash movement over his left eyebrow to indicate where James had reported he had a scar. "James Melbourne," she repeated. She spread her hands out over her audience as if she was covering them, and then put her arm up and flexed her muscle, pointing to her bicep. "James Melbourne will protect you," she said. "James Melbourne good."

"James Mellon goot," replied the leader.

"James Melbourne good," Jane said, then looked at each of her men, asking them with her eyes to repeat the phrase.

They understood and joined her, "James. Melbourne. Good," the three said.

The natives looked at one another, then back at her, and said haltingly, "James Melbourne goot?"

Jane glanced at her men and nodded, wordlessly letting them know, 'repeat please.'

"James. Melbourne. Good," she and her men chorused determinedly.

The native men responded just as forcefully, "James. Melbourne. Good!"

"And I do believe that we just started a legend," Jim said

softly, a wide grin of satisfaction erasing his earlier insecurity.

***

"Weel, if I wasna seein' it with my own eyes, I wouldna believe it. James Melbourne! How've ye been?" Benji said, the tears welling up in his eyes as he spotted his fellow time traveler straight ahead.

James was bent over a log, both hands employing a rough stone as a hatchet, whacking away with an overhead chop, trying to de-limb a burnt branch from a sturdy eucalyptus tree that had apparently been knocked down by lightning.

James looked up, stunned and speechless. His jaw dropped open in amazement as he slowly stood up straight. He didn't move another muscle until he felt the drool slip down the side of his chin. He closed his mouth and wiped the slobber with the back of his sap-stained, dusty hand.

"Benji?" he whispered, afraid that others might hear him speak to the apparition. He had hallucinated before, but only of Leah and their children. This had to be Benji, though, didn't it? Could he be imagining his friend—a rescue from his horrid predicament—out of desperation and hunger?

"Aye, it's me, Benji. Of course, ye remember Wee Janie. She's my wife now. And we brought another friend, but more about him later. Are ye ailin' there, man?"

"Yes and no. I mean, no and yes. I mean," James took a deep breath to try to compose himself. This was not a dream, but what should he say? Well, just answer the question, he told himself, shaking his head slightly to tell the other voices in his head to be still.

"I'm not hurt. Much. It's just that I haven't been eating enough lately. The water is sour and the fish and shellfish I manage to share with the others doesn't always stay in me. I'm salvaging charcoal so I can sweeten the water. That should quell half my problems. But...but," James broke down, the tears streaming down his face as he rushed into the big, red-headed man's open arms, "I missed you... I mean my family... I mean, hell, everyone."

"There, there," Benji soothed, as he stroked the top of James's dirty, matted hair. He looked down and saw that clumps of it were falling out—probably due to malnutrition, he surmised. "We brought ye a bit of food and a few packets of seeds. Ye should be able to get back in shape in no time. Oh, and we also brought a wee medical kit. I made sure to put in some vitamins fer ye in case ye werena eatin' right. After all, I dinna think they had parritch and tomatoes here. At least yet," he added with a wink.

"Have you heard from or seen Leah and the children? Are they okay? And Jody and Sarah? Wallace and Evie, and…"

Benji held up his hand and nodded his head, asking James wordlessly to calm down. "I havena seen them since I saw ye in '83, but I ken they're fine. And now that ye have a bit of help, includin' one of those fine Leatherman tools I added to yer care packet, some strike-anywhere matches and vegetable seeds, I'm sure ye'll be able to handle anythin' that comes yer way. Ye'll be fine now, I'm sure."

James took a deep breath to compose himself before speaking. His prayers had been answered. "I'm sure it will, God willing. Australia was—is, I guess—a nation started by convicts, marines, and sailors. From what I remember of history and hearing firsthand accounts from my mates, the convicts were mostly poor people who committed petty crimes. Most lost their jobs to the Industrial Revolution—they were starving, stealing food or clothes, just trying to survive. Their real crime was being born poor in a time where the British government felt it easier to ship them away— transported beyond the seas for their natural lives—rather than train them with new skills. I'm sure with these new treasures," James held up the parcel Benji had given him, "life will be easier for all of us first generation Aussies. And our new friends."

He nodded to the small cluster of natives who were watching from behind the bushes, a cautious twenty feet away. "The Aborigines are clever and resourceful. I don't want to 'domesticate' them. Most of us just want to live here in harmony, side by side with them. I'm sure if I stay out of their way, they'll stay out of mine. They're very territorial, after all. I've noticed something strange, though. They treat me with an unusually high regard, almost as if I were a king."

"James Melbourne good," Benji said with a thick Aboriginal accent, then smiled.

"Hey, how did you know that's what they said?" James asked.

"Because my clever wife taught it to them the first time we were here. That was a few centuries ago geologically speaking, but only a few minutes ago by the clock in my belly," he said, then laughed at his growling stomach. "Oh, and your great-grandson here provided the visual demonstration of who they were looking for. Janie jest let the men ken that 'James Melbourne good' looked jest like him only smaller," Benji said, employing the same sign language Janie had used, then pointed to Jim.

"You're my great-grandson?" James asked in awe, his head tipped up at the man with his familiar features, but an unusually large body size.

"Aye, and there are at least a few greats on the grandson, too. The family sticks around here, Grandpa. I was born in Sydney in 1985. Thanks fer comin' over and survivin'."

"Well, thanks for coming back and saving me. How'd you do it?" James asked.

Jim shifted his shoulders, uncomfortable with recalling his scariest memory. "Ye see, a couple days ago, the MacLeod males—they're not worthy of bein' called men—had just come and kidnapped my wife and son, right under my nose. And me bein' a cop! My bright wife, Becky, tossed my son—he's a James Melbourne, too, by the way—to Janie here.

"I wanted to chase them down. But my daughter Bibby has 'the sight' and said I needed to read the letter that came in the box we had jest received. One had 'read me first' scrawled on the outside of it, so we did. In it, ye told me and Benji to rescue my wife at Swona Island, at an old house with a red door, and to hurry up and spare no expense."

Jim shrugged his shoulder and grinned, remembering the happy ending. "So we did, came home and read the other letters, and here we are."

"So, there's another Bibby Melbourne?" James asked.

"And two Jim Melbournes—me and my son."

"And Bibby has 'the sight'?" James asked, his eyes wide in shock.

"Most definitely. She had it before she could walk or talk. I hear her great-grandmother, Leah Melbourne, had it, too. By the way, she comes over here to be with ye in June of 1790 and brings yer three children with her," Jim said with a big smile. "Aye, I have to go back to my family—my 21st century family—but I wanted to let ye ken that yer wife, my great-granny, will be comin' over to stay with ye. I dinna ken if they liked Australia more than North Carolina or if it jest cost too much fer ye all to travel back, but ye'll all be fine."

"Spoken like a true believer," Benji said, then thumped Jim on the back. "It dinna take ye too long to believe."

"No, it took me over two hundred years, at least. I'm sorry I was so stubborn."

"Well, don't worry about it, son. I think your stubbornness is hereditary. If I wasn't so pig-headed—or determined, depending on how I'm feeling about myself at the moment—I wouldn't have survived this far nor would my family." James sighed and shook his head. "Just over a year to wait. I'd better get busy and build them a place to stay."

"Oh, and here's a gift from yer brother. Billy got with yer dentist in England. He had him build these based on yer old dental x-rays and some photos that yer da had. There's a little kit in there so ye can build up the palate as needed. It's sort of a build yer own denture kit. Ye told us in the second letter that ye had lost yer two front teeth to a combination of poor nutrition and brawling. Now ye willna scare yer family the first time they see ye."

James took the plastic container and opened it gingerly. He couldn't help but gasp at the morbid but glorious contents: a partial plate with two front teeth. "All I want for Chrithmath ith my two front teeth," he sang softly, not even trying to contain his lisp. "Thanks, mates," he said, his face turned up to show the tears that he thought he'd never have again.

Tears of joy.

Chapter 7
Lousy Timing

Elizabeth Farm, named after Elizabeth Macarthur, wife of wool pioneer and early Australian statesman John Macarthur, is an historic estate located in Rosehill, a suburb of Sydney, New South Wales, Australia. It is Australia's oldest surviving European dwelling and the site of the earliest successful farm settlement.

Present day

"Mister Simon, I can't just stop this shuttle in the middle of the tour and take you back. You'll have to wait until we get to our next stop. From there, you can hop off and catch one of the other buses. Our company prides itself on accommodating diverse and eclectic groups of tourists," the tour guide said.

"Hmph! As I said earlier, when you repeated the same information in a slightly different manner, my name is *Master* Simon," he said, then plopped back down and grabbed both ends of his seatbelt. *Click. Magnificent! I got it on the first try this time.*

Marty Melbourne stifled a chuckle, then turned to Bella and confided, "Actually, I'm glad we're going to Elizabeth Farm. I wouldn't doubt my son spent a bit of time there at some point." His eyes brightened up at the possibility. "Maybe there'll be a record of it."

Simon leaned forward and glared at Marty, reminding him that he shouldn't be so chatty lest he let slip that if his missing son visited the area, it would have been over two hundred years in the past!

Acknowledging his traveling companion's tacit reprimand with a quick nod, Marty turned and looked out the window, trying to ignore what he knew in his heart: he'd never see his youngest son again. But just in case, he'd try one more time.

When they pulled to a stop, Bella thumped Artie on the soles of his feet. "Wake up, Prince Charming."

Artie sputtered unintelligible half-sentences, unable to complete a thought before another one came out. He rubbed his eyes, taking deep breaths to clear his head, then sat up and looked around, re-orienting himself to where he was. And why.

Marty let himself out of the van before the driver came around, ready to assist young Bella and the others. She took his hand, followed by Artie who stepped out and offered his hand to help Simon get out. If it was possible, and it was, the short-legged man growled at young Artie.

"Ho-kay," Artie muttered and rescinded his offer. "Bella, I'll be back in a minute." He looked around, spotted the restrooms, then added, "Don't leave without me."

Before he could dart off, Bella gave him a quick hug of excitement, then kissed him on the cheek with sincere gratitude. They were getting so close! They would soon have the bottle and Phoebe would be free. Master Simon was sure to have it on his person, which meant that before long, Artie would make it hers.

Artie glanced at the tourist information help desk and grabbed a shiny flyer and pen as he passed, barely able to contain his grin of excitement. *She likes me! She likes me for who I am, not how much I can get her, or even for being a helping hand to get her sister away from Lionel. As if that jealous wench would ever leave Lionel's side!*

Artie slipped in the family restroom and locked the door. He took out the fancy blue facet-cut glass bottle he had pinched from Simon's pocket as the grumpy old man got off the bus, then reached in his cargo pants pocket and took out the empty and well-scrubbed small bottle that had previously contained milk of magnesia. He uncapped it and made sure it didn't smell or have anything in it. Still clean as the day he'd sanitized it.

And now for the *pièce de résistance*: the Fountain of Youth elixir—time in a little blue bottle.

"Hello again," he said softly. "Thanks for saving my life, even if I overdosed and rejuvenated a few years. I'll return you undiminished and unpolluted in just a few moments, but I have to take your jacket, as it were. Lionel wanted that little blue bottle, but he didn't specify that the contents had to be original. I'll put together a custom blend for him."

Tearing off the edge of the flyer, Artie rolled the triangular-shaped scrap into an impromptu funnel. He carefully poured the Fountain of Youth elixir into the clean travel-sized bottle, then tossed the scrap of paper into the trash. He sniffed his fingers, then hazarded a small lick. "Nope. No spills. I'm already younger than I want to be."

Artie turned on the faucet, poured a dribble of coffee from the cup he took out of the trash into the fancy cut blue bottle, then added water until it was completely full. "And he thought he'd only get a partial bottle." He shook his head. *Sorry, big brother, but you don't deserve the real stuff. Maybe I didn't either, but death biting at my butt caused me to be a little desperate. Maybe returning this to Simon instead of giving it to you for your selfish reasons will erase some of my bad karma. At least, I hope it does.*

He scribbled on the remains of the peeled-off label on the store-bought bottle containing the true youth elixir and stuck the real bottle with the *faux* contents into his pocket. Time for a plant. That would be easy. Trying to convince Bella that her sister was using her and had never been in distress was going to be the real—and more difficult—trick.

"Oh, crap!"

Ready to leave, Artie opened the door, but quickly closed it again. The two goons, E.I. and Levi, were here. They must have taken a taxi. They were staring at the restroom door, waiting for him to leave. There weren't any alternate escape routes, either—no windows or other doors. Maybe he could slip out unseen if someone would create a diversion…

And there she was, knocking on the door softly. "Are you all right? Bella asked.

Artie cracked the door open and whispered, "I need you to start yelling at me. Give me hell about something."

"What do you mean you lost my ring down the toilet?" Bella shouted, her loud, angry screech just inches from Artie's ear. "I told you I could take care of it myself, but nooo," she added, even louder, "oh-so-smart husband has to try and get the permanent marker off it for me."

Bella paused, waiting for more instructions.

Oh, yeah…she wants me to tell her what to do next. "Keep hollering at me when I come out," he whispered, "and hit me, too, but not too hard."

Artie opened the door, his hands up, ready for the assault. "I'm sorry, dear. I truly am. I…"

"What do you mean?" Bella screamed, swinging her backpack at him, her voice railing at him even louder.

Artie sneaked a quick look around the room, spotted Marty and Master Simon, and started backing toward them, leading the argument dance toward Simon so he could return the pilfered product. "I have insurance on the ring," he said, then pivoted around the tall interior house plant. He rushed to Simon's side, slipped the bottle into the distracted man's pocket, then added, "At least, I'm pretty sure I took out insurance on it when I bought it."

"What?" she exclaimed and pummeled him again with the

backpack. "You don't know whether it was insured or not?"

"I know they offered it to me, but I can't remember…"

"So, you're both stupid *and* cheap?" she screeched. "How'd I ever wind up with such a loser?"

Artie caught the question in her eye: *Is this enough or do I need to keep going?*

He raised his eyebrows, letting her know the deed had been done. "Darling," he said, and neared her, his hand out to calm her with a gentle shoulder caress, "if I marry you all over again, will that make it up to you? A new ring, ceremony, the works?"

Bella grinned, a true smirk of devilish satisfaction beaming. "A new proposal, too?"

Artie got down on one knee, looked around at the crowd, and shouted, "Hey, everyone. Watch this!" *There's no way E.I. and Levi can hurt or kidnap either one of us if we're grandstanding.*

"Isabella, my dear. Would you marry me? Again? I want to spend our lives together; whether in sickness or in health; whether in good times like vacationing in a foreign country, or bad times like I accidentally flushed your one-carat wedding ring down the toilet; for richer like maybe we'll win the Irish

Sweepstakes, or poorer like we can't even get a pauper's pass for food; but most certainly, forever and ever?"

"Yes! Yes!" the crowd yelled. "Tell him yes!"

"Yes, Artie, I'll marry you," Bella said, blinking back the unexpected tears at hearing such a passionate proposal.

"Again or for the first time?" Artie whispered, looking deep into her soul to see if she was still acting or if she could tell that he had been sincere and was she answering his question truthfully.

"Kiss him! Kiss him!" several female tourists shouted.

"Way to go!" hollered the tour bus driver.

"You're done for now, dude," commented the young man in bike shorts, then whispered to Marty, "but I wouldn't have minded some of that myself."

"First time," she moved close, a sly smile on her face. "Any time," she said, and gave him a quick peck of a kiss.

"That's not a kiss," the bicycle rider hollered. "You can do better than that!"

She turned her head toward the cyclist and said, "You bet I can," then turned to Artie. "Every time," and kissed him as if no one was near, as if Artie really was her Prince Charming and would help her escape…

Artie felt her entire body tense, her warm deep kiss suddenly cold and mechanical, like he was kissing a gumball dispenser. He pulled back slightly, enough to appear as if he was still smooching, but asked her, "What's wrong?" rather than whisper affections.

"Why are we doing this?" she whispered, then brought up one leg for him to grab.

The two continued the ruse but were now both acting instead of reacting. "The goons," he said softly, then spun her around so he could see where they were. "Crap. Gone. Done."

Bella pulled away, then straightened her shirt and smoothed back her hair. "That's all for today, folks," she said. "He apologized, I forgave him, and we're ready to start all over again. Here, here to new beginnings!"

"I'll drink to that," the bus driver said, and grabbed a bar patron's beer and saluted the couple. "Too bad I'll have to wait, but I'll drink to you two when my shift is over." He returned the bottle to the drinker and asked, "Do I get to kiss the bride?"

"Nope," Artie said, and pulled her close. "I'm not sharing."

"Oh, yes you are," E.I. said, and grabbed Bella's arm.

Levi came up behind Artie and brought his meaty hand up between the pseudo-groom and his terrified make-believe bride, separating the two with the quick uppercut. "We missed you, lad. I hope you have what we want. Lionel told us where to find you."

"No, he didn't," Artie hissed. "Don't try and con me. And let go of my wife!"

"Is there a problem?" the biker asked, the bus driver coming up beside him for support.

Artie looked at Bella, wincing in pain as the grinning E.I. clutched her arm tighter, her flesh squeezed tight.

"There better not be," Artie said. "Let go of her and you'll get what you want."

"All right, but I want to kiss the bride, too," Levi said. He leaned in, determined to steal a kiss, then quickly pulled back and grabbed Bella's wrist as she brought her hand up to slap his lip-puckering face away. "Oh, you shouldn't have tried that, Missy."

"Let go of the lady," Marty said, his hand on Levi's arm, a gentle suggestion rather than a forceful blow. "You have a crowd of people here and no one wants to watch me take you out," he said, and added a wink.

"Oh, puh-lease," Levi snorted, but let go of Bella. He turned to Artie. "You'd best come outside and give me what I'm after. She's probably a lousy kisser, anyhow."

"The couple will come and go as they please. They have nothing that belongs to you, so leave them be," the deep voice boomed.

Cleveland had arrived.

No one had seen the tall copper-skinned man with golden dreadlocks enter the building, but they were definitely aware of him now. Eyes bulged and jaws dropped as both men and women stared at the magnificent creature who had one protective hand on Bella's shoulder, the other on Artie's.

Bella and Artie looked up. "Cleveland?" she asked.

"Who?" Artie mouthed to her then slipped out from under Cleveland's hand and clutched her close.

Cleveland winked at Bella. *Your husband can take care of you. It's time for me to take out the trash.* He turned to the two confused thugs. "You haven't left yet, Esau Isaiah?" he mocked. "And what business do you have here, Levi Isaiah?"

"How did you know my name?" E.I. asked. "Nobody but my mother knows my name."

"Yeah, or that we have the same last name," Levi added.

"Having the same last name tends to happen with twin brothers," Cleveland said, "Even fraternal twins."

Levi and E.I. looked at each other and shook their heads. "Phoebe. She must have sent him after us," Levi said.

"Actually, I did," Elvis said, as he walked out from behind Cleveland. "Word on the street was you were out to harass this young lady who was just out to save her sister." Elvis shook his head. "Even if she didn't need or want saving."

Mark Twain stepped forward from Cleveland's other side. "And without letting Phoebe know her sister would be in harm's way when retrieving the little blue bottle, you took money from Lionel for the same thing plus got a bonus to get rid of his little brother. Airfare to Australia isn't cheap and the two of you got paid by both Phoebe and Lionel—that's twice—for taking the same contract plus the travel expenses. That's called double dipping your drumstick in the sauce where I come from," Twain said, then looked up to Cleveland. "Thanks for letting me say my piece. They're all yours."

"Wait! What?" E.I. sputtered as he looked up to the colossal Adonis with the menacing smile. "What'd we do and where are you taking us?"

"I'm taking you two brothers to meet the Three Sisters.

You have heard of the Three Sisters, haven't you?" Cleveland asked, one hand on each of the brother's shoulders, his grip strong enough to let them know he was in charge, but not so powerful that they were bent over in pain.

"You mean that formation in the Blue Mountains?" Levi asked, his tongue flicking across his lips nervously. "Yeah, I saw them once. We don't need to see them again. Hey, E.I. Isn't our flight leaving in just a couple hours?"

"Don't worry about catching your flight," Cleveland said. "I'm your travel coordinator today. You'll go where I take you and like it. After I have a bite or two for lunch."

Cleveland turned to the group of spectators. "Enjoy your tour of Elizabeth Farm," he said, then turned to Marty. "And I think you'll find something interesting in the patio area. There's a water device that may be of interest to you." He squeezed just a bit harder and urged E.I. and Levi forward toward the door.

"My driver will take us in my limo. It's much faster than the bus."

Bella was stunned. Even though she hated the two goons, just the thought that they might be sucked dry by a vampire in a few moments gave her the shivers.

"Are you all right?" Artie asked, then wrapped both arms around her and hugged her close. When she didn't respond, he took her hand and said, "Let's go outside and get you warmed up. Besides, I'd like to look around. I'm curious about what he wants Marty to see."

"Yeah, sure..." she said, and moved along with him, stunned. So much had just happened. It was safer to block out the extreme range of emotions she just been tugged through rather than react to any of them. Shock, the human body's coping mechanism. Right now, she welcomed the numbness. At least she had Artie to take care of her.

Once they were alone, Artie whispered, "I got it! I got the bottle!" He took his excitement down a notch when he saw she was still in stun or shock or whatever it was called. She truly was young and innocent. No matter what that man Cleveland had planned for E.I. and Levi, he hoped he caused them pain in the process. He'd been their punching bag for too many years, too small in body to fight back effectively, smart enough to know he should curl up on the ground and assume his 'Worthless' persona so Lionel would tire of the exhibition and go on to other distractions. Suddenly, he had no sympathy for the pair. *I hope that guy's a cannibal and gnaws on their leg bones like drumsticks.*

"Is she all right?" Marty asked Artie. "Let's get her out in the sunlight. Here, give her a drink of water, too."

Artie accepted the canteen and tipped it to Bella's mouth, a trickle spilling over her bottom lip before she started to drink on her own. "Thanks," she said, coming out of her daze. "I didn't realize I was thirsty. Hey, is that an old drinking fountain?" she asked, then moved over to the huge cube of granite with a birdbath-looking sink in the top.

Marty looked at his flyer and read off the details. "This dripstone was originally used at Vineyard, a neighboring estate... Bella? What's wrong? You look like you've seen a ghost?"

Bella was squatted beside the wooden frame, examining the limestone structure, one hand gliding over the bottom to feel for an artisan's signature. "I think I found it. I can't tell what it is, though. Artie, give me that phone for a minute."

Artie dug through the backpack and found the phone Cleveland had 'gifted' him at the airport. Hopefully, it was charged and Bella could figure out how to use it.

She tapped and swiped the screen and opened the camera app. "This ought to do it." She felt for the engraving again, then held the phone down and away from it. "I hope it's not too close to focus." *Click! Click!*

"What'd you find?" Marty asked, leaning over her shoulder to see. *Was this what Cleveland had been referring to?*

"Let me try again," Bella said, then assumed the position once more, this time the back of her hand on the ground so she could get a larger area photographed. *Click! Click!*

She held the phone close so only she could see it. "Did James ever go by the name Jim?" she asked Marty.

Marty bit his bottom lip and shook his head, then brightened up, his radiant smile erasing his frown. "But his middle name is Ignatius! His initials are J.I.M. Is that what you found?"

Bella brought the phone close to Marty and showed him the screen. "Looks like your son was here," she whispered in his ear. "But I think it was a long time ago. Was he a fairy?"

Mouth twitching side to side, trying to contain the laugh at the term and his shout of discovery at the same time, Marty gave up. "Yes, he was! Is! Whatever!" He turned to Simon, ready to share the good news with someone who could appreciate it, when he realized he had gone over the top—again—with his excitement. "Can we go to the portal now?"

he asked. "The one closest to here?"

"Not yet," Simon said, his eyes fixed on Artie. "I have a little business to conclude first."

"Before we start our chit chat," Artie said, "Let's go over to the trees," nodding to the crepe myrtles, exploding in hot pink blooms.

Simon pulled up his collar, despite the heat. "As long as the bees aren't biting," he mumbled.

"Stinging," Bella corrected, "Bees sting, not bite, and these are probably honey bees, so they won't bother you."

She was smiling now. Her emotional funk had evaporated with the influx of new topics to consider: time travel and the Fountain of Youth water. She took Artie's hand, and led the way. "Come on, husband. Let's get this settled once and for all."

"Before you say anything, Master Simon," Artie said, "I'd like you to check your pockets. You might have...ahem...overlooked something."

Simon glared at the youth. *He planted it back on me!* He checked all his pockets, pulling out and inspecting various packets and colored vials, confirming he had the potions and dry blends he had left London with, then patted himself down just to make sure he hadn't missed something. "No, not what I was looking for."

Artie lunged forward, ready to frisk the disgruntled man himself, when Bella stepped in front of him.

"Are you looking for this?" she asked, producing the facet-cut blue bottle, "or this?" She reached into the backpack Artie held and showed Simon the blue milk of magnesia bottle. She turned it over and looked at what was written on the front. She hadn't seen the personalized message when she had swiped it during one of the first times Artie had hugged her. She giggled, then handed it to Simon. "I think this is the one you want," she said.

Simon snapped it out of her hand and twisted off the cap, sniffing the contents and ignoring the container. His cheeks lifted and mouth widened as he smiled, an unfamiliar facial contortion for the centuries-old man. "The sweetest smell on earth," he said and recapped it.

"Aren't you going to read the label?" Marty asked.

"It's not important," Simon said, "but if it will make you feel better." He held the bottle two feet in front of his face and squinted. "Sorry. Wort."

"I wouldn't have pinched it if I had a choice. I don't know if anyone is ever truly ready to die, at least before a few hairs have turned gray. I guess what I'm trying to say is, I owe you a favor, big time. Or little time. Whatever you need that is mine to give—or something that's not mine but I can acquire—let me know."

"No, no, no. Wait," Bella said. "So, you're not a teenager? And you stole this," she held up the original facet cut blue bottle and wiggled it back and forth, "how many years ago?"

Artie looked at Simon for confirmation. "I believe it was eight years ago, right?"

"Did we miss something?" Elvis asked as he walked up to the gathering, a picnic basket in one hand, Mark Twain following behind him with a pitcher of sweet tea.

"I was just about to enlighten these young travelers about the importance of these," Simon took the fancy bottle from Bella and held it up next to the other blue container. "Just in case you missed that lecture, too, I'll give you the abbreviated version.

"This bottle and its contents—and the knowledge of where to source it—is a secret too dear to be handled by the common man. Our group has been the keepers of the secret for..." Simon thought about the still boyish King Tut, "millennia."

"But what about the fairy part, the time travel?" Bella asked.

"There are two aspects of time—one relative to one's own self, as in aging. The other, a person's relationship to the rest of the world. Let me explain. There are time portals all over the world, their accessibility easy for one traveling back in time. Airplanes fly all day and night in the 21st century and beyond, after all. You can't manipulate location, at least in this realm, but you fold time, slip through the creases, so to speak, from one date to another.

"The other—the personal side of time—can be controlled with this sweet tonic, naturally trickling forth from The Fountain of Youth. I'm sure you've heard of it, how it's been sought after for millennia, the search for it the reason the New World—the Western Hemisphere—was discovered. Its properties are volatile, easily dissipated in daylight. Many have found its source over the years but never discovered its properties because they didn't know this one important fact: it must *first* be contained in a blue glass bottle to be effective. Think of the blue light as the catalyst needed to both release the water's properties and keep it active."

Artie swallowed his bite of sandwich and asked, "So, if a man—or woman—had access to this sweet elixir of life and had the map of all known time portals, he or she could be eternally healthy and wealthy? Hmph. Too bad wisdom doesn't come with the package."

"But what about him?" Bella asked, looking at Elvis, bored with the lecture and now inside, preening in front of his reflection in the glass display case containing vintage looking glasses.

"The masters groom others, making use of their knowledge of appealing to the masses from their time eras. All these men were special in their own times—worshipped and idolized. It's not an accident that you recognize many of them. Occasionally, they mix in—maybe swap places with an actor or impersonator in a one-man show—so they can refuel their desire and appreciation of the adoring crowds, rejuvenate their pheromones, maybe even go so far as to..."

He paused, shrugging his shoulders in discomfort, wishing he had never brought up that aspect of interacting with citizens from the local time era.

"Do a little procreating?" Bella asked.

Simon nodded, blushing scarlet, his fop sweat returning.

"Here," Marty said, handing Master Simon his own fresh handkerchief, "I think she knows enough. And, I've learned a lot more, too."

Marty pulled Simon aside. "I've never been famous or renowned, and I never hoped to be. I just wanted to make sure my son was all right. Now that I know he made it to Australia, I feel better, but I still want to see him and hug him one more time." *And maybe bring him and his family home.*

"All right. Take one of those maps from the credenza and I'll show you where we need to go. It's your task to find a driver."

Simon took the cup of sweet tea Artie offered him and sighed. Between the long flight and this Melbourne man's tenacious drive to find his son, this had to be the longest day he'd ever endured.

Chapter 8
Lost Again

Somewhere between Port Jackson and the Blue Mountains
Now and then

"I just hired a man to take us to the edge of the preserve. You did say the spot was near here, right?" Marty asked, pointing to the spot on the colorful tourist map.

"Don't worry about those stories about Blackheath," their grizzled driver told them, misunderstanding their discussion. "It's only been a couple of women who disappeared from that old house. And they was probably half crazy before they went in." He laughed cruelly. "And after they got out, a fistful of Valium and a couple bottles of hair color took care of the rants and the rapid aging they supposedly experienced."

Marty looked at Simon to see his reaction.

None.

At least, at first. Slowly, but surely, Simon's already thin lips disappeared into his face, his words contained, but his angry grimace evident.

The driver pulled to a spot at the side of the road. "Ah,

they were probably just trying to drum up attention so they could tell their story and drink free beers. Now, see that rock with the white cross marked on it? That's where I'll pick you up. I come by here every day at this time, so if you decide to spend more time out in the bush, I'll catch up with you the next day. I even come out on Sundays."

"Thanks for the ride," Marty said, and handed him the fare plus a fifty-dollar tip. "I'll see you in a day or two."

"Right..." he said and sped away. *Let's see if my bird's still on a winning streak. Even if he isn't, my cut of the gate will be a handsome bit. Cockfighting may be illegal, but it's always profitable when you have the right venue! Maybe I'll be back tomorrow, maybe next week...*

"You go that way," Simon said, then looked up at the sun and squinted. "And I'll go this way."

"No, no, no," Marty said, his panic barely contained. "You said you'd escort me. I...um...tend to get lost, you see."

"Open your map," Simon said, not even trying to contain his exasperation. Now that he was in Australia, he had a few of his own research projects to investigate.

Marty opened the map and set it on the rock with the white cross. Simon pointed to a spot and said, "It's right there," then turned to leave.

"Normally, that'd be fine, but I don't know where we are without a 'You are here' arrow. Where are we?"

Simon shook his head. How did this man ever get this far in life? He pulled out his fountain pen and marked a big X, then circled the spot he had pointed to.

"All right. That'll work for me. Will I see you again?" Marty asked.

"Hmph. Nothing is certain in this life. Be well, and I hope you get to see your youngest son again."

Simon felt a chill, suddenly filled with dread. With all the hoopla about the missing elixir, he had forgotten Cleveland's warning about the Melbourne Legacy. He looked inward, searched for his reserve of compassion, and broke off a piece.

"Mar-ty," he said, uncomfortable using a familiar name instead of a title, "I hope you know that your son was a very important person in the development and success of this country. It is imperative that he remain in the 18th century. It wouldn't be wise to try and convince him otherwise."

A nervous chuckle escaped before Marty covered it with a joke. "What? You think I might put a rift in the time space continuum or something? This isn't a science fiction movie, you know."

"Be that as it may, I think your son already made his decision on where he wanted to live with his family. I would advise letting him be his own man, not his father's son. This is his legacy."

Marty's shoulders slumped in defeat. "Yes, you're right. But I still want to see him one more time, if I can…" He looked up at the sun as Simon had earlier, wondering if that made a difference in the southern hemisphere, too. When he looked back down, the man was gone.

"Where did he go? Why did he leave so soon? Oh, well. Onward and onward."

Ten minutes later, Marty put the drachma he had been rubbing nervously back in his pocket and took out the map. He looked closely at the marks Simon had made. "This map is more confusing than the first one," he mused aloud, spooking the kookaburra bird with his sudden verbalization.

"*Guu guu bur rah,*" the bird answered, as if he were giving his opinion on the situation. The brown and blue bird canted his oversized head side to side, trying to figure out what the large, pale-colored, oddly plumed creature with the strange call was.

Marty looked up and snorted a quick laugh at his exotic avian companion perched a scant ten feet away. "I think he's still mad that I stole his map," Marty said. "I told him several times I was sorry and even gave him back the original. Of course, I made a copy for myself first, but dang!" Marty held the magnifying glass over the lower right edge of his new map, hovering it over the area Simon had marked.

"He said there was a portal around here somewhere, but I can't find it."

Marty reached into his vest pocket and took out a photograph printed on what appeared to be linen. "And who's this Wiley Waldo fellow he gave me a picture of before we left England? Good Lord, what happened to him? I mean, this Aborigine bloke looks like he got hit with about *six* ugly sticks."

Marty folded up the fabric photo and swapped it for the compass in his vest. He looked up at the sky. "Hmph, I can get lost in the southern hemisphere just as easily as I can in England or America. And this compass is worthless; it's spinning all over the place." Marty stuck it back into his vest pocket, then pulled it out again quickly. "Good grief! It's spinning because of the erratic magnetic fields. I'm here! Can I have a hallelujah, anyone?" he called up to the sky.

"Guu guu bur rah, guu guu bur rah," replied the bird, as if on cue.

"Why, thank you very much, Mr. Kookaburra," Marty said, and bowed to the source of the noise in the tree. "Would you care to join me on the hunt for Waldo? I believe he's the man to lead me to James and the other First Fleeters."

The bird flew out of the tree, skimmed a mere two feet above Marty's head, then screeched his call to a black man standing on one leg, maintaining his balance with a walking stick, a grin spreading from one cauliflower ear to the other.

It looked as if Waldo had found Marty.

Gulp.

Marty swallowed his initial fear, stood tall, and then extended his right hand in greeting. "G'day, mate," he intoned with an Aussie accent.

"James Melbourne goot?" Waldo asked as he ventured closer, his walking stick now grasped with both hands, holding it diagonally across his body defensively.

"Wait, what?"

Waldo pursed his lips in exasperation and repeated,

slower this time, "James. Melbourne. Goot?" He dropped one hand from his roughly-hewn sapling and walked slowly around Marty, standing six feet away, poking him with his stick to be sure he was solid and not a specter.

"No, I'm not James, but I am a Melbourne. Does that count?" he asked brightly, trying to hide his rapidly increasing fear.

Waldo grunted, then stabbed his stick into the ground in an aggravated manner. He approached Marty suspiciously, wearing only his scowl of determination. He moved in so close that Marty saw that what he thought were muddy smears on the naked man's skin were actually the remains of fish entrails.

Marty's stomach churned. He didn't know whether it was from fear or the stench, but either way, the gurgle was loud.

Waldo poked him in the gut with his gnarly index finger and smiled broadly. Silently.

Marty quickly raced through his knowledge of these people. The Eora weren't cannibals; they were fish eaters, shellfish harvesters, wild flora and fauna gatherers. He sighed in relief. *You've come this far, Marty. Don't let him spook you. He's not testing you for tenderness.*

Now Waldo was completely invading Marty's personal space, barely an inch away from the much taller and woolen-clothed—and now very frightened—white man. He grunted and bared his teeth in a non-menacing grimace.

Marty looked side-to-side, wondering if this was a signal to Waldo's mates to join in.

Nope. They were alone.

Waldo grunted again, then returned to his broad, toothy smile.

"When in Rome..." Marty mumbled, then returned the same idiotic grin.

"Hmph!" Waldo's investigative grin disappeared. He shook his head, grabbed his spear, and walked away into the brush, leaving Marty wide-eyed with wonder.

"What the...?" Marty mumbled. "Well, if I was supposed to know what that meant, I guess I would. Now, where is that rascal Simon? Whether he wants to help or not, I need him as my guide. He said James would be here with the other First Fleeters. I know there were around 1500 convicts, marines, and sailors who came over, but one naked Aborigine isn't exactly what I call civilization."

***

Three days and two canteens of water later, Marty still hadn't found James or Simon. He had, however, learned from the last time he was lost: he had marked the trees along the way.

"Won't get lost again," he said aloud. "Or at least, I won't lose track of my time portal." He pulled his compass out of his pocket to verify his location.

"Guu guu bur rah. Guu guu bur rah."

"Well, hello again to you, too, my friend." Marty subconsciously clutched his stomach, then realized what he had done. The queasy tummy verified what his compass and nocked trees also said: he was at the time portal.

"I guess it's time to say good-bye, Mr. Kookaburra. I had hoped to see my son again, but I guess it just wasn't meant to be. I'm sure Simon made it back to wherever it was he wanted to be. Now it's time for me to return to my lovely bride and my other son and his family. Maybe in a few centuries, we'll come back for a visit. By then, this area will have roads and working GPS's. Until then, *adieu.*"

And with that, Marty clutched his drilled Greek drachma, shut his eyes and focused on the image of his wife, Bibb the First, then peeked out as he walked between the two

132

shredded-bark eucalyptus trees.

James was going to make it without his help. He had already confirmed that in the letter he had written...and by giving him plenty of descendants. He chuckled. His great-great grandchildren so many times over by James were the same age as son Billy's child, Mac.

It looked like the Melbourne line wasn't going to die out, after all.

Chapter 9
Let's Say I Do

"It seems so empty now," Bella said, looking around the living museum at the dozen school children picnicking under the tree where Elvis and Mark Twain had been just half an hour earlier.

"What? I can see over thirty people without even turning my head. That's not counting everyone in the other rooms, in the garden..." Artie stopped when he realized what she meant.

Their adventure was over.

Or could be.

"You do realize that your sister is no longer in danger, that Simon has his elixir returned, you discovered a major clue so your fairy buddy could go time-traveling back to who-knows-when to see his son, plus we don't have to worry about the goons anymore."

"I'm pretty sure Cleveland had fun with those two. I hope they don't mess with his cholesterol levels."

"What are you talking about?" Artie asked.

She leaned over and whispered, "He's a vampire. But I think he's one of the good guys and only dines on the creeps. I guess blood is blood, though, unless the dine-ee has been drinking."

Artie laughed and said, "Yeah, *Goon au vin*."

Bella chuckled at his joke, then stopped abruptly. "I guess we're done, too," she said, then sniffed back the tear she'd been trying to keep in check since Elvis and Twain had left.

"What? You and me over and done with?"

Bella nodded, sure that if she tried to talk, she'd lose it completely and start blubbering.

"I don't think so, darlin'," Artie said, lifting her chin to look her in the eye. "My proposal was sincere, even if we didn't get to seal it with a true kiss because E.I. and Levi showed up. I'm willing to spend the rest of my life with you if you can handle having a husband who still has six inches grow."

She looked at his crotch and giggled.

"No, dear. Up here. My eighteenth year, I grew six inches taller. As far as the other…well, let's go get a real marriage license then check it out. I don't want to frighten you."

"But how do you know you want to be married to me? We only just met?"

"In my thirty years of life, one thing I've learned is that a person's true personality comes out under stress. Plus, we already learned how to trust one another, what essentials are needed in life—a blanket, water, and a couple of granola bars—and how to kiss. I want to marry you today, so you can't change your mind."

Artie reached into the backpack and pulled out the envelope stuffed with charge cards that had mysteriously appeared when Cleveland had come to their rescue at the terminal. "I'm sure Cleveland wouldn't mind if we used these and got you a ring and took a proper honeymoon. After all, he did give us his permission to be happy."

Bella pulled up her shoulders and giggled. "Imagine that: blessed by a vampire."

"And schooled with Elvis and Mark Twain. I can't imagine what will come next."

Bella bent forward, her forehead pressed to his. "As long as we're experiencing it together, I'm sure it will be great."

"Kiss me," he said.

"Every day for the rest of our lives. Fulfill my fantasies."

The End

A Note from the Author

Thank you for reading *Time in a Little Blue Bottle*, the 'transition' novella between The Fairies Saga series and the upcoming series Fairies Down Under, the tales of the time traveler who sails with The First Fleet out of Great Britain and helps establish Australia in 1788.

I'd appreciate it if you took a moment and left a review on Goodreads and/or Amazon. Your impressions on the story may help others decide whether this story is a good fit for their tastes.

If you're interested in the other books or projects I'm working on, please sign up for Time Travelers Anonymous - my newsletter (http://bit.ly/2DHnews) and follow me on Goodreads (http://bit.ly/2DHgdrds) and BookBub (http://bit.ly/BBDani).

Other books by Dani Haviland

<u>A Stingray Christmas</u>: (First book in the Arlie Undercover series) Anchorage detective on medical leave travels from Alaska to Arizona to see for the first time the son he'd fathered as an anonymous sperm donor. Great and rotten surprises await the cop with the smartest smartphone around.

<u>The Biggest Heart Ever</u>: (Book two in the Arlie Undercover series) When would Arlie learn that trying to do everything by himself could be deadly—and make Charlene a widow before they were married?

<u>Always a Bigger Fish</u>: (Book three in the Arlie Undercover series) Back in Alaska, Arlie finds out he's a target. Will vacationing detective Billy Burke (from THE FAIRIES SAGA) have information to help nab the scalper?

THE FAIRIES SAGA SERIES (in order with novellas):

<u>Naked in the Winter Wind</u>: (lengthy novel) How does an older woman wind up as a young hottie in Revolutionary War era North Carolina? First book in the time travel series.

<u>Ha'Penny Jenny</u>: (historical novella) More about the naïve and psychic young girl who was adopted into a time traveling family. Will her past catch up to her?

<u>Aye, I am a Fairy</u>: (lengthy novel) Young British lord finds himself entwined with a time traveling family and must decide if he should go back in time, too. Second book in the series.

<u>Dances Naked</u>: (novel) Directionally challenged time traveler is rescued by Cherokee in 18th century. What must he do before the chief will show him to The Trees, the portal through time?

<u>Chasing Christmas</u>: (historical novella) A young Cherokee is rescued from an abusive man and changes the lives of many in this 18th century America family.

<u>The Great Big Fairy</u>: (lengthy novel) Very tall Benji grew up in the 20th century but was born in the 18th. When he finds a way to return to his grandparents in the distant past, he goes for it. Once there, he realizes he can't stay, but must return to the future. Fourth book in the series.

<u>Little Bear and the Ladies</u>: (historical novella) What's a bachelor trapper to do with all the females he rescues from the Hessian mercenaries? He'd better hurry and figure something!

<u>Little Drummer Boy</u>: (historical novella) Young Scout works to earn money for a home in post-Revolutionary War America but runs up against prejudices and snowstorms.

<u>Never Too Young</u>: (historical novella) Scout and Ha'Penny Jenny have grown up, but will they be able to spend their life together, or will the past and ruffians get in their way?

CONTEMPORARY NOVELLAS – BENJI, THE LOST YEARS

<u>Luke the Unexpected</u>: Love of classic motorcycles brought them together, but Luke and Holly have other challenges to face. Find out how their friend Benji got his stripes here.

<u>Pool Boy Wanted: No Experience Preferred</u> (rather racy) Young Benji has been a hostage and slave, but life gets worse when an older woman decides she wants him as her own.

STAND ALONE NOVELLA

<u>Kit Kringle: An Alaskan Tale</u> (contemporary) Kay moved to Alaska for the wrong reasons, then decided to stay and start her own business. What she hadn't planned on were prejudices and falling in love.

<u>Be My Angel</u> (contemporary) Wyatt's dream to help save the wild horses in the west started with buying a rundown ranch in western Oregon. What he hadn't anticipated was being mesmerized by a sassy woman in a wheelchair.

 Dani Haviland has never been one to believe, "You can't do that!" She started her own business in 1994, selling tractor parts in Alaska, then segued to writing and publishing books, becoming a *USA Today* bestselling author in the process. She currently splits her time between Alaska and Oregon, tirelessly writing and gardening, publishing and promoting, while claiming to be 'retired.'

Contact

Website: www.danihaviland.com

Twitter: @dani_haviland

Facebook: Dani Haviland Author *or* The Fairies Saga Fans

Amazon: http://bit.ly/dhAuthor

BookBub: http://bit.ly/BBDani

Goodreads: http://bit.ly/2DHgdrds

email: dani@danihaviland.com

www.ingramcontent.com/pod-product-compliance
Lightning Source LLC
Chambersburg PA
CBHW082012170626
46817CB00009B/3068